MW01135528

# They Called Her Strawberry

Written by: KC Marks

"Warn all the haters,

I'm getting ready to work that thing.

Warn all of your enemies,

I'm getting ready to work that thing.

I'm not responsible for what God gave you,

I'm responsible for what He gave me.

And if I perceive it to be mine,

Don't get mad when I work what He gave me."

Bishop TD Jakes

Foreword

Sex, politics, and murder, I wonder why this story has not been written? Perhaps it is because everyone that has tried to tell this story thus far has unequivocally been silenced. Some have lost their jobs and some walked away with millions in hush money. One may have even lost her life.

The secrets and truth died with the woman named Tamara Greene, whom they called Strawberry. Her murder has never been solved, although I hope and pray that justice will be served on those who put greed and their own careers above the value of a human life.

Media capitalized on her murder in numerous articles and newscasts. They described her in such a way that devalued her as a person. Headlines read, *"Stripper Slain"*, or *"Exotic Dancer Gunned Down"*. They never reported that she was a beloved child and a beloved mother. That is what she was, a person. A person who deserved dignity in life and in death; no matter what she did for a living.

She was rumored to have danced at the Manoogian Mansion, for none other than the mayor of Detroit at the time, Kwame Kilpatrick. Mike Cox, the attorney general at the time, said that the party did not take place. It was an 'urban legend'. This can't be substantiated; the hospital records from Detroit Receiving Hospital disappeared. Mayoral security staff escorted her that night, with injuries from a beating that was supposedly rendered at the hands of Kwame's wife, Carlita Kilpatrick. Rumor has it that she came home to find a party going on and her husband in a compromising position with the dancer that they called Strawberry. It was a very untidy situation for a husband; especially for one who was also a politician.

The bullet that killed her was from a .40 caliber Glock pistol. That was the standard police issued hand gun in the Metro Detroit Police Department at that time. The three Detroit Homicide Detectives who initially investigated her murder were demoted. Their notes on the investigation disappeared. As did Tamara's cellular phone, the video of her funeral, signed statements, and other assorted physical evidence that had been collected. The computers housing the investigative notes were wiped clean and eventually confiscated completely from both the Internal Affairs and Homicide departments. The file was then moved to cold case prematurely and without meeting the criteria.

To say that sloppy was the accepted standard, in this case, would be a liberal and generous statement. Due process was not followed in the handling of the evidence. Nor was it followed in the transfers and demotions of officers who investigated her murder. No one was held accountable for these unethical and unprofessional incidents, each a crime. At best, removing evidence from a murder file was obstructing justice. At worst, it was a conspiracy to cover-up for a murderer. All participants in thwarting the investigation were accomplices in a serious crime. Covering up a murder in the first degree is as serious as it gets.

Urban legends historically are tales intertwined with threads of fact, fiction, and a touch of local folklore to make them interesting and believable. Woven together delicately they create a strong fabric that stands the test of time. Much like an old quilt, the story is passed down through many generations. It is my hope that this tale, this urban legend recounted, will keep the memory of Tamara Greene, the woman they called Strawberry, alive.

The compilation of each article written in the last several years has added layer upon layer to the vivid image in my head of the possibilities of how things. "*Could have*" happened.

Nothing will be alluded to or told; that has not been made public by other sources, which will be listed in depth at the end of this book. I am making no allegations that have not already been made publically and formally, most being several years ago, without contest, recant or lawsuit.

That being said, *maybe* the story went like this.......

Chapter 1.

The Party

It was early September, 2002 in Detroit. At the All Star Lounge on Eight Mile Road, the manager, Jerry, had called two of his dancers, Strawberry and Nikki, over to his usual perch at the end of the bar for a talk.

He stirred his fourth mixed drink of the night; took a long drink from it, then he asked both of them, "Are either of you girls available to work at a private party tomorrow night?"

Strawberry looked at him and thought, *this dude has more chins than a Chinese phonebook.* She smiled and asked him, "What does it pay?"

Usually she didn't like parties unless they were VIP's. She knew that she could make more cash working at the club on a Friday night. Nursing school happened to be expensive. Money was not *a* concern; it was *the* concern. Nikki lit a cigarette and blew the smoke off to one side, away from their faces. Both of the girls looked at him and waited for the answer.

Jerry looked exasperated. "You'll both make a grand, you interested or not? They asked for my best girls, that's why I'm asking you two."

Strawberry smiled sweetly and replied in a sugary tone, "Of course I'm available. What about you Nikki?"

Nikki's eyes flashed to Strawberry as she answered the question, "Yeah I can work; but I'm going to need a ride. My car took a dump yesterday and Darrell ain't about to drive me all over town."

With a nod of her head, Strawberry confirmed that she would give her a ride. The manager looked at them and said, "It's best if you two ride together anyway. Keep the details about this on the down-low. I need you both at the Manoogian Mansion for a bachelor party. Be there no later than 6 P.M."

Strawberry tossed her head to the side, winked at him and said, "Ok, boss, and speaking of work, I need to get back to it. Some friends of mine just came in and I can tell they want to buy me a drink."

Nikki and Strawberry laughed and walked away as the manager picked up his cell phone. Strawberry overheard him tell someone, "Yeah, it's all set; they'll be there at 6 o'clock sharp. Just let me know if you need another girl."

Business picked up at the club for the rest of the evening and neither dancer thought much about the party they were scheduled to work the following night. Hours on end of entertaining inebriated men had both of them worn out by the end of the evening. Strawberry offered Nikki a ride home while they were changing back into their street clothes. They were quiet as the bouncer walked them out of the club. Side-stepping the trash on the side-walk, they made their way around the building. Strawberry handed a homeless man a brown paper bag, on her way, as she walked to her car. He was there most every night, slumped over on the sidewalk, Nikki watched him as he opened the bag, held up a sandwich in a shaky hand and nodded, saying something that sounded like, "ta-ta."

Strawberry smiled at him like he was the most important man in the world and told him, "Curtis, you know I wouldn't forget about you."

He flashed a toothless grin in her direction; then quickly turned his attention to the sandwich he held in his hands.

The ride home was short and uneventful the streets were deserted at that time of night. Both of the girls just wanted hot showers and soft beds. It was 4 A.M.

The following morning Strawberry awoke to a blaring alarm. She stumbled out of bed and tripped over a pile of clothes as she made her way to the coffee pot in the kitchen. She started her coffee, turned on the hallway light, walked into her son's room and said, "Rise and shine, boy-o-mine, it's finally Friday."

He groaned, "Ten more minutes mom, puuuhhh-leeassse."

"Come on, sleepyhead, you can sleep in tomorrow as late as you want. The bus will be here in twenty minutes, time to get them lazy bones movin'."

She made him some oatmeal for breakfast as he got dressed and decided that she would go back to bed once she got him on the bus. She turned the coffee pot back off without pouring a cup and dug around in her purse for his lunch money.

After she laid it on the table she told him, "Your dad will pick you up after school, I have to work tonight."

"Ok. Dad said he might take me to a Tiger game this weekend anyway! Did you know Matt Anderson can throw a fast- pitch ninety-seven miles an hour? That's why they call him *the heat*."

"I didn't know that. C'mon, get your jacket or you'll miss your bus. Want a pop-tart for the bus ride?"

"No, I'm full. It's not cold out, mom. I don't need a jacket."

Grabbing the jacket from where it was hanging on the back of the chair, she held it out to him, "Take it anyway; you might need it at your dads this weekend."

He shrugged as he took it from her hands, "M-kay"

He tossed the jacket over his shoulder and swiped the money from the counter and put it in his front pocket. Then he grabbed his book bag from the chair and headed toward the door.

"Ok, honey have a great day, I love you."

"I love you too, mom."

She watched him from the window as he stood at the bus stop, turning away only after he was securely on the bus. She turned the deadbolt on the door and went back to bed and slept soundly until the early afternoon hours.

When she had awaken; she looked at her phone and noticed she that had four missed calls. Three of them were from bill collectors and she made a mental note to sit down Sunday and write out some checks. She was grateful that she had scheduled that party that night. She could definitely use the money. There was one message from the manager of the club that reminded her that she needed to be on time and confirmed the directions to the Manoogian Mansion. She jotted down the directions, deleted the messages and sat down with a fresh cup of coffee in front of the television.

After surfing through the channels and realizing there was nothing on worth watching, she popped in a VCR tape of TD Jakes, 'Get ready, get ready, get ready.' His positive message, as usual, uplifted her. It made her feel like good things were just around the corner and that she mattered. He would never know that he was the inspirational voice that led her back to school. 'Slap three people and tell them, "I'm moving forward." Repeating after him was automatic to her. The words; "I'm moving forward," reverberated off the walls of her empty living room, as she slapped her throw pillows. She believed with every fiber of her being that she was moving forward. She had plans, big plans for a better life.

A few hours later she gathered up her work clothes and set them beside the duffel bag she used for work. After she showered she sat back down on her sofa and watched Dr. Phil dispense advice to a victim of domestic violence. Interested in the program and caught up in the story, she forgot that she intended to touch-up her pedicure until the news came on at five o'clock. She grabbed the polish from the coffee table and quickly applied it. *Shit, this isn't going to have long enough to dry.* After carefully sliding her feet into leather braided flip-flops, she grabbed her purse, her duffel bag and her keys and headed out the door a few minutes after five thirty. Once she had the door locked, she hit the trunk button on her key fob, tossed her duffel bag full of gear in her trunk and headed over to Nikki's.

She called Nikki from her cell phone and let her know that she was on the way. Nikki had better be ready to go when she got there or they would be late. Jerry would bitch them out for sure if they weren't on time. He had made such a big deal about it. Everyone had their quirks and that was his. Girls could be drunk on the job and he wouldn't say a word. But if someone showed up late for work more than twice a week, he would send them back home for the night and tell them, "If you wanted to work, you would have showed up on time."

She pulled in the driveway of a duplex on Evergreen where Nikki had been staying with her new boyfriend and tooted the horn with a couple of short blasts. The door for the downstairs unit opened almost immediately. Nikki held up one finger and the door shut just as quickly. A few minutes later she came out with her duffel bag and Strawberry popped the trunk for her. She threw her bag in the trunk and started to get into the car with a cigarette and Strawberry said, "Uh-uh, not in the car."

Nikki took one last long drag, then she flicked her cigarette halfway across the yard, "Sorry, I forgot."

Strawberry wanted to tell her that the filter of her cigarette butt was not biodegradable. It would never go away unless someone picked it up and threw it away, but she figured, "Why bother? She probably doesn't give a shit anyway." So she said nothing, backed out of the driveway and headed toward the eastside. Nikki settled in for the ride and tried to find something good on the radio. She settled on Usher:

*Tell me, do you wanna' get freaky?*
*I'll freak you right, I will….I'll freak you right, I will*
*I'll freak you like no one has ever made you feel*

She looked at Strawberry and said, "Guuuurrrl, don't you know I'm excited about tonight? If they like us we might get some more gigs out there. I wonder who is going to be there."

Strawberry turned the car onto Dwight St. and told her, "I couldn't care less; I'll just be glad when I finish nursing school and can put this job behind me. As long as they've got the money to make it rain on me tonight, I don't care if it's the president and Jay Z in there."

Nikki laughed, "I hear ya' girl."

They pulled up the long driveway toward the mansion and Strawberry commented to Nikki, "Wow, look at all of the cars, we should have a good night. Are you ready to rock this par-tay?"

Someone formal looking directed them where to park. He had a radio clipped to one side of his belt and a gun holstered to the other. Strawberry noticed the badge on his jacket had the letters E.P.U., she figured that was mayoral police security. They gathered their bags from the trunk and followed him into the house through a side door. It must have been an old service entrance. There were caterers in crisp white uniforms rushing in and out. They carried massive silver trays with shrimp on ice, finger appetizers and assorted cakes and pastries. They were being lead by another uniformed officer to a door further down the hall that she assumed was a kitchen.

He escorted them into a large, elegantly appointed powder-room; "You girls can get ready in here. The caterers have been instructed not to come in here. They have a separate bathroom. Once you get changed, go left, down the hall - until you get to the last set of double doors on the right-side, that's where the party is."

Strawberry had already figured that out by the noise and the cigar-smoke that was wafting through the air, "All right, we'll see you in a bit."

He winked, smiled lewdly and opened the door to let go out, "I'll be seeing *you* in a bit."

Strawberry smiled at him and thought, *well aren't you original? I can't wait to take all of your little money.* After he walked out of the room she reached into her purse and pulled out her bottle of Xanax.

She removed two peach-colored pills from the bottle and offered one to Nikki, which she gladly took, "Thanks girl. Man, this place is something else."

Snapping her black fishnet garter stockings into place, Strawberry replied, "It sure is. Can you imagine living here?"

Nikki was applying false eyelashes with a steady practiced hand, "It would be like living in a museum. It's nice, but it ain't homey."

Strawberry looked around the formal looking powder room with gold gilded mirrors and marble tile. The mansion *was* fantastic. She was putting on pink-tinted lip-gloss when another dancer was brought in. Strawberry had never seen her before. She was dressed in a police officers' uniform. Strawberry and Nikki's eyes met in the mirror and as they did, they raised their eyebrows to each other without commenting. *You see some strange things in this line of work, that's for sure.* The new dancer wasted no time getting ready and by the time Strawberry had finished freshening up her make-up all three of the girls were ready for work. The last thing the dancers put on was their four-inch heeled shoes. They then walked through the house to where the party was. Their heels clicked on the imported travertine floor in perfect unison.

They entered the room full of men and as they did someone put a mixed compact disc into the stereo and the music started pumping through the atmosphere. Aretha Franklin's voice belted through a state of the art sound system as they each headed to a different area of the room,

*What you want, baby, I got it*
*What you need? You know I got it*
*All I'm askin' is for a little respect when you get home*
*When you get home*
*Re-re-re-re-re-re-re-spect, just a little bit, just a little bit*

By the time the first jam had finished playing, it was clear that everyone had loosened up significantly. Smoke rolled through the large room as more current hip-hop music blared from the speakers. The costumes that the dancers had been wearing hit the floor before the second song had finished. The noise level had risen. A few men still tried to hold conversations that inevitably had to be continued at another place and a later time. Nikki had singled out the bachelor and sat him in a chair in the middle of the room and had commanded his full interest within a matter of seconds. The girls were professionals and had taken the party to another level, as they had been hired to do. DMX started blasting through the house;

*"Y'all gon' make me lose my mind, up in here, up in here*
*Y'all gon' make me go all out, up in here, up in here*
*Y'all gon' make me act a fool, up in here, up in here*
*Y'all gon' make me lose my cool up in here, up in here"*

The party went on and as the men got more inebriated, it got raunchier and louder. Everyone was plenty high, the music was pumping and the girls were only wearing heels and a smile. One of them put on a show in the center of the room; straddling a chair, as the other two were giving lap dances. Quite unexpectedly, bright lights flashed on overhead. Every eye in the room switched gears. Their gazes shifted away from the dancers and moved, wide-eyed, toward a commotion in the front vestibule.

A crystal-shattering woman's voice screamed, "What the hell's going on in here?"

It was long seconds before anyone registered what was happening. The most powerful men in Detroit were stunned. Before they realized what was going on, Carlita, the mayors' wife, had left the room and re-entered it wielding something that resembled a baseball bat swinging wildly. She blasted Strawberry in the arm like she was knocking one out of the park. After she struck Strawberry several times, then she turned and hit Nikki in the face with the bat. All the while, she was screaming, "Get the hell out of here! Get out! Get out!!"

Blood spurted out of Nikki's nose, all over the travertine tile, and Strawberry scrambled for her clothes.

One of the security guards wrestled the bat away from Carlita. She pointed her finger toward the mayor's face and yelled, "I told you, not in my house! Get these bitches out of my house!"

Then she turned her fury toward the third dancer and pummeled her in the head with both of her arms flying like windmills.

Strawberry watched as the other dancer crouched, turned and grabbed the radio from the belt of the nearest security guard. She yelled into the radio; "Officer down, assistance needed at the Manoogian Mansion on Dwight! I repeat, officer down! "

The officer reacted by snatching his radio back from her hands, "Are you crazy? What the fuck is the matter with you?"

After a brief struggle, one of the security officers restrained Carlita by grabbing her from behind in a bear hug that encircled both of her arms. She kicked at his shins wildly, screeching, "Let me go! Get these bitches out of my house now!"

It was extremely chaotic. The mayor was trying to calm his wife down. He assured her, "I'm getting them out of here right now. You need to calm your ass down. You just caused one big-ass problem."

His words just ticked her off all the more, "I caused a problem? You brought naked women in my home, in our children's home... and I'm the one who caused the problem? Are you out of your damn mind?"

One of the security officers was barking out orders, trying to get some kind of control of the situation. Strawberry heard him tell one of the guys to get their bags and another one to go pull three cars around front. He managed to escort all of the dancers from the house through the front door into different SUV's that had appeared within seconds. All three of them were still naked, except for their heels, and they had all sustained injuries. Nikki's face was still spurting blood and Strawberry was bleeding from the side of her head and she could barely move her arm.

The security guard who had been bossing everyone around slid into the driver's seat of the SUV. Strawberry started in on him immediately, "I want my clothes, I want my car, let me out of here. Where are you taking Nikki? "

He turned from the driver's seat of the SUV and told her, "Look, you need to calm down. I just sent someone in for your clothes. "

She watched as one of the other security guys went in through the side door. He came back out a few seconds later with three bags. Once he had distributed the belongings properly he ran back in and came out with a blanket for her to wrap up in.

He *must* have been a police officer because the walkie-talkie thing on his belt was crackling and announcing that emergency

24

responders were en-route to the mayor's address, possible officer down.

She over-heard him clearly say into the two-way radio, "Cancel the responders, there is no incident at that address. Officers are on the scene."

She covered up with the blanket and shivered. Her brave words didn't match her actions; "You need to let me out of this vehicle right now."

He turned back to her again, "We're going to take you to get that arm looked at. I assure you we will have your car dropped off at your house. But right now we are going to make sure you're ok."

Her eyes shot daggers at him. "Where's Nikki?"

An Irritated look was on his face, "We are taking her to get looked at too. Let's not make a bigger deal out of this than it is."

Sick of his arrogant, bossy attitude, she replied, "Were you born this much of an asshole or did you have to practice to get that good?"

Once the SUV was in motion and headed toward the hospital, she just stared out of the window. She realized that she had no other choice. They had decided for her what she needed. Her arm was throbbing and medical attention *was* a good idea. But she didn't like anyone taking her car or making choices for her. The entire night had turned into a freaking nightmare. The driver of the SUV pulled into a gas station, the other two SUV's pulled in behind him. They parked by the air machines, away from the pumps. The drivers all got out and talked to each other. Strawberry tried to listen to what they said but couldn't hear them very well. An ambulance pulled into the gas station parking lot as she was digging in her bag with her good arm, trying to find some clothes to put on. She saw Nikki get out and tell the ambulance workers that the mayor's wife had just beaten the hell out of them.

Her driver pointed to the other SUV and told Nikki, "Get your ass back in that car. We're taking you to the damn hospital."

Strawberry rolled down the window so she could hear them better. The driver of the other SUV had his hand on Nikki's arm, escorting her back into the vehicle.

She heard Nikki say, "Get your fucking hands off of me!"

He opened the back passenger door and firmly guided her friend back into the vehicle, "Get in."

The ambulance driver stared at him, with a look of disbelief on his face. He asked her driver, "Are you sure that none of them have injuries that require immediate attention?"

Her driver seemed to be the head dick-in-charge, "I told them to cancel the emergency response call immediately after it was made. We don't need ambulatory services. You can leave."

The ambulance driver looked in Strawberry's direction and saw that she had the window down and asked her, "Do you need an ambulance?

He was a nice looking man. Strawberry guessed him to be around thirty. He looked good in his white uniform. Crisp and clean, like fresh new sheets.

Shaking her head side to side she said, "No," in a barely audible voice.

Her driver piped in, "It looks like they all have minor injuries. We are taking them to the hospital right now to get checked out. You can follow one of us if you like, but they are all going to be treated at different hospitals. We are headed to Detroit Receiving, they're headed to St. John's and that one is going to Providence." He pointed to each of the vehicles as he told the ambulance driver which hospitals they were headed to.

The ambulance driver didn't look impressed with his plan, "We'll follow you to Detroit Receiving. Let's get going."

Everyone got back into the vehicles and each of the dancers was driven to a different hospital. During the ride Strawberry had somehow managed to struggle back into her yoga pants and tank top, not bothering with a bra or panties. The SUV driver made no comment as his eyes flashed back and forth from the road to his mirror, watching her as she got dressed. The ambulance followed behind them with its emergency lights flashing. Within minutes they had pulled up to the emergency entrance of Detroit Receiving Hospital. The ambulance driver pulled in directly behind them.

He jumped out of his vehicle and told the driver of the SUV, "We can take it from here."

The driver responded, "I'll go with her."

He looked at him like he would've liked to punch his lights out, "We have privacy laws. The only way you are going in there, is if she wants you." Then he looked at her, "Do you want him in there when you see the doctor?"

There was no hesitation in her response, "Hell, no!"

He pointed to the sign that said 'waiting room '. Then he told the security guard, "You're going to have to wait in there."

The ambulance driver used his identification card that was on a clip attached to his belt and swiped it through a reader by large steel double- doors. They automatically opened for them and he led her through the entryway into the Triage unit. A nurse pointed in the direction of an empty room with the tip of her pen, indicating that was where he should take her.  Strawberry let out a long sigh of relief. She didn't like that driver guy one damn bit.

She looked at him, "Thank you for everything."

He helped her onto the examination table, letting her use his arm for balance, "Looks like you had a pretty rough night. Someone should be in shortly to have a look at you. Do you want me to get you something to drink or anything before I go?"

Strawberry looked at him gratefully; "No, I'm ok. Thanks again, I really appreciate your help."

She told the doctor and nurses the truth about what had happened. That she had sustained her injuries at the hands of the mayor's wife. First they bandaged the laceration on her forehead. After they finished with that they sent her to get an x-ray of her arm, to make sure that it wasn't fractured.  Once that had been confirmed, they put it in a sling and told her that she needed to ice it and take it easy for a few weeks.  Her shoulder was bruised and that would take some times to heal properly.  The doctor told her that once the swelling went down, it shouldn't be so painful to move her arm. They gave her a prescription for thirty Vicodin and twenty Flexeril. Before she left they advised her to follow up with her family doctor in a week to ten days.

When she walked into the waiting room the mayor's security guards rose to their feet. The driver asked her, "All set?"

She had to wonder if his big-ass buddy was a deaf mute. He hadn't said a word; "Yes, where's my car?"

They started walking toward the exit. He pointed to the parking lot on the left, "This way. Your car is already at your house. I have your keys and an extra thousand dollars for all of your trouble."

Every time he opened his mouth he made her angrier. It was more his smug, superior manner than the actual words he used. She couldn't help quipping, "So that's what it pays, a thousand dollars to let the mayor's wife beat the crap out of you?"

He clicked the key-fob that he already held in his hand and unlocked the waiting SUV, "It's in the best interest of everyone to keep this as quiet as possible. No one could have anticipated what happened tonight. Cut the drama-queen act, shit happens."

What a douche-bag. She looked out the window and said nothing as they drove her home. There were ten one hundred dollar bills sitting on the seat beside her. As she placed the money in her wallet the words, "damage control," flashed through her mind. Damage control is the phrase they used in politics. It sounds so much classier than the truth.

When they arrived at her home, the driver got out and stepped around the car to her side; opened the door for her and reached in to help her get out.

When he reached for her, she jerked away and told him, "Don't you touch me. Don't even lay one finger on me. Get the hell away from me. "

He threw his hands into the air in mock surrender, backed up and smugly said, "I was just trying to help you."

She grabbed her bag with her good arm as she scooted to get out of the vehicle, "Fuck you, and you."

Exhausted and groggy from the shot of Demoral; she dragged herself up to her door, dropped her bag on the porch with a thud, and unlocked it. After she struggled to get her bag through the door for a few seconds she was finally able to get the door closed, and shut those bastards out of her world. She fell back on the door for a second then reached up for the deadbolt lock. Once it was clicked into place she let out a ragged sigh. Then she slowly made her way through the living room and went straight into her bedroom. When she finally reached her bed, she collapsed into it and pulled the blankets tight around her.

She shut her eyes as the scene played out again and again in her mind. The shot was wearing off. If she moved around very much, it hurt, so she tried to remain as still as she could. She laid in bed in deep thought about what had happened that night for a long time. Daylight had started to seep through the curtains of her dirt-filmed window before sleep and exhaustion finally claimed her.

Chapter 2.

Jerry Quite Contrary

She woke up at 4 P.M. the following day to the sound of someone banging on her front door. She slowly made her way to the door. After she figured out who it was, she opened the door. There stood the manager from the club, looking sheepish. She invited him in and sat down on the sofa.

He didn't look like he was comfortable in his skin; he tugged at his collar awkwardly and stood there by her door looking at her like he didn't know what to say.

Even though he saw her naked every night, she was uncomfortable to be dressed in only her robe. Strawberry was a persona that existed only at work, and she left her there. It was just a role she played to pay the bills. Tamara pulled her robe together in the front to cover her-self a little more and asked him, "Jerry, would you mind getting me a glass of water? My arm is throbbing and I need to take a pain pill."

After he had taken a few steps into the kitchen he turned and asked her, "Glasses?"

"They're up in the cupboard to the right of the sink."

The tap water ran for a few seconds while he waited for it to get as cold as possible for her. The ice tray was empty, so he removed it from the freezer and sat it on the counter. Directly on top of the papers they had given her from the hospital the night before. At least he tried. He gave her the glass of water and took a seat in the black-leather recliner that was opposite her and waited for her while she took her pill. She winced with pain and wanted nothing more than to go climb back into her comfortable bed.

Jerry perched on the edge of the chair and said, "Look, you aren't going to report this to anyone are you?"

She closed her eyes and leaned her head back against the sofa and thought about what an asshole he could be sometimes. Then she slowly opened her eyes, looked at him steadily and told him sarcastically, "Yeah, I will probably be ok, thanks for asking."

He stared at a non-existing spot on the carpet with flushed cheeks. At least he had the decency to look ashamed, "I'm sorry about what happened."

Tamara wasn't letting him off the hook, "As for if I report it or not, it's none of your damn business."

At that statement, Jerry wrinkled his forehead and looked at her in a concerned manner and told her in a low tone, "I understand you're hurt, but these are people that you don't want to piss off. Why do you think I'm here? I was told to pay you a visit and nip this in the bud. It's better for you to just let this whole thing go."

Tamara was pissed. Someone sent him over here to threaten her? Who the fuck did these people think that they were? Let it go?

She glared at him through swollen discolored eyes, "I think you need to leave. My medicine hasn't started working yet and I'm not in the mood for any company right now."

Jerry got up and walked to the door, "You need to think about what I said. I don't want you to get hurt any worse than you already are. Don't do anything foolish"

Tamara asked him, "Is that a threat? It sounded like one. "

His voice had a trace of exasperation when he said, "You don't get that I'm trying to help you?"

Her reply was curt, cold and as close to professional as she could muster; "I appreciate all of your concern. I'll give you a call when I'm ready to come back to work."

His brows lifted as he told her, "You do that. Hope you feel better soon." He opened the door and let himself out of her apartment without saying another word.

Tamara needed to talk to someone. She sat for a long time after he left and deliberated about who to call. She felt so alone and her whole body ached. She decided to call big-mama, her grandmother in Alabama. Big-mama always knew what to do and talking to her always made her feel better, no matter what.

Big-mama answered on the third ring, "Chile', I was just gonna call you. I've been thinking about you all day. I woke up in the night thinking about you. What's going on? You all-raght, baby-girl?"

Hearing her grandmother's voice was all she needed to let it out. She sobbed into the phone. She cried and told her grandmother everything that had happened.

Once she had gotten the whole story out her grandmother said to her quietly and purposefully, "Chile', I told you no good was going to come from that dancing. I knew some fella's wife was going to cause some real trouble one day, but no one, and I mean no one, has the right to beat you with a bat."

She reached for a Kleenex and blew her nose loudly, "I know mama."

Big-mama went on to say, "I raised you up on my knee tellin' you 'bout Rosa Parks. Tellin' you, don't be afraid to take a stand. Right is right. You wasn't raised up to let no one treat you second class, whether you was dancing or not."

"I know mama."

"Do you think for one minute Rosa would let that high-fallutin' woman beat the crap outta' her and not make a report? The woman had a right to be mad, at him! He's the one she should've beat down, not you! Right is right chile', ya'all don't want me to forget I'm a Christian and bring my old ass up there to see about this mess."

Tamara smiled, "You don't have to come up here, mama."

"I will, I'll bring my own security. They won't fool with me."

Big-mama was usually a boisterous woman. Everyone in the family always said it wasn't when big-mama yelled, it was when she got real quiet and spoke so a person could hardly hear her. That's when it was time to get worried, that's when we all knew she was good and mad. Tamara knew what she meant when she said she'd bring her own security too. She didn't play around. A pearl handled derringer lay by her heart, safely tucked into her bra. And she wasn't afraid to pull it out.

"No, you don't need to come up here. You're right as usual, and I knew you would tell me the right thing, I already knew in my heart what I need to do. That's why I called you. I knew you would tell me. I promise, when I get feeling better in a little while I'll go downtown to file that complaint."

Big-mama said,"Ok, chile', you make sure you call me when you get home, I don't care what time it is, I'll be waiting to hear from you. You be careful, you heah' me, Tammy? You call me the minute you git' home."

Her grandmother rarely called her Tammy. She promised she would call her back later that evening and laid the phone on the coffee table and promptly fell back asleep on the sofa. The Flexeril made her sluggish, but together with the Vicodin it did help ease the pain.

Chapter 3.

The Report

Several hours later she woke up to the sound of her cell phone ringing.

It was Nikki, "Hey girl, how are you doing?"

She glanced at the clock on her VCR as she said, "I'm actually getting ready to ride downtown and file a report about what happened."

"For real?"

Sitting up, she replied, "Yes, for real. My arm is really sore and I know I'm not going to be able to work for a few days."

"Oh."

Pointedly she asked Nikki, "How are you? Do you want me to pick you up on my way to the police station?"

Nikki seemed to fumble with her words, "Wow... um.... No..... I don't think that is such a great idea. I'm actually feeling fine."

"So that's it? She gets to do that to us?"

Nikki changed the subject, "Girl, there's been a black car outside of my house all day. I think it's an unmarked police car."

Tamara pulled her curtains to the side just enough to peer outside of her apartment, "I think your imagination is running away with you. But I understand if you don't want to press charges."

Nikki sounded relieved to be off the hook about going with her when she said, "I doubt they will even question her about it."

The retort tumbled out of Tamara's lips, before she even had time to think, "Of course they won't. If it had been one of us who beat the hell out of her, we'd already be locked up."

"The issue she has is with her man, if you ask me."

"Everybody in this town knows he is hotter than a two-peckered billy-goat." Both the girls laughed into the phone.

The line went silent for a few seconds; then Nikki s voice changed, "I'm not crazy, there is a car out there and I think he is watching my house."

Her tone became even more serious as she went on to say, "Listen to me, Tammy, I know that bitch hit you, and I know it hurt, but the police ain't going to do one damn thing about it. She's the mayor's wife. If you say anything about what happened, you are just going to make problems for yourself."

"You're not the first person to tell me that."

Nikki ignored her attempt at dry wit and went on, "Did you know Jerry came by here? I didn't even know that fat-ass knew where I lived.""

"Yeah, he came by here too. I wasn't in the mood to watch him sweat all over my furniture and threaten me about not making a report. I really don't like people telling me what to do. I'm getting tired of being pressured not to tell on little-black Princess-Freaking-Di. I can barely move my arm. I'm going to make a report just as soon as we get off the phone. I'm not going to be bossed around after getting beat up."

Nikki paused for a second, before she replied, "Well, be careful girl. I'm just saying."

"I'll call you later."

Tamara pressed the end call button on her phone and sat it down while she dressed and got her things together to take downtown. She gathered up the emergency room records from the night before, including two Polaroid photos showing her injuries under her shirt. After shoving everything into an oversized bag she grabbed her keys from the table. As she turned the dead-bolt, unlocked the door and stepped out onto the porch the hairs on the back of her neck and arms started to rise. The fall air rushed in and surrounded her with a cold burst. It felt like fear and permeated her bones instantly. As she walked to her car she pulled her bag close to her body.

As she stood at the door of her car, her hand on the handle, she turned her head and looked back to the street. Tamara watched as police car slowly drove up the street. It seemed to her like he drove deliberate and slow. The driver focused his gaze on her when he passed by. She thought; *everyone is going bat-shit crazy with the paranoia and now what? Me too?* She started her car and cranked her radio almost as loud as it would go to shake off that weird doom-like feeling and she headed downtown. Bare

Naked Ladies would normally put her in a good mood, but it wasn't working that day, so she turned it up even louder and sang with them at the top of her lungs:

*"We've got these chains, hanging around our necks.*

*They wanna' strangle us with them, before we take our first breath.*

*Afraid of change, afraid of staying the same,*

*When temptation comes, we just look away."*

Before she knew it, she was downtown. The parking structure was almost full, so she had to circle twice to find a spot that was open and that wasn't reserved. She walked into the precinct and waited for someone to take her report. She looked around and wondered how these people worked in this piss-hole. It stank like a mixture of vomit, diapers and Mad-dog 20/20. Shabby chairs with stains and tears. Filthy coffee cups sitting on the desks. The institutional tiled floor had faded to a dull gray. Bleak eyes of a man being booked stared at her as she sat and waited. By his matted hair and raggedy appearance she guessed him to be homeless. She gave him a half smile as she thought, *poor old fella', he's probably hungry.* Finally a female officer called her name. She stood up and followed her down a long

hallway to where her desk was located. She opened a dented up

grey metal file cabinet and retrieved a complaint form from a

green file-folder and proceeded to ask her some questions.

"What is your full name?"

"Tamara Greene."

"Date of birth?

"4/27/74"

"When did this incident happen? "

"Night before last"

"Can you tell me what happened?"

"I was performing at the Manoogian mansion as a dancer at a

bachelor party. I'm registered to the city as a dancer under the

professional name, "Strawberry". While performing at the

mansion, the mayor's wife came in unexpectedly and beat me up.

Me and two other dancers, I think one was a cop. Security

Officers that work for the mayor took us all - different hospitals.

EMS workers met us a gas station by the mansion and followed us to Detroit Receiving hospital. I want to file an assault charge. I brought my records from the doctor. I'm going to have to take at least a few days off work because of my injuries. Verify it with the 911 records. I know someone called 911; I heard it over the radios of the mayor's security people"

The officer taking the report almost choked on her coffee, "You are making some very serious allegations here, Ms. Greene. I'm going to need to make a copy of these medical records." The smell of garlic almost turned the air purple over her head as it escaped with her words. The thought popped into her mind, *finally this bitch looked at me.*

"What I am making is a report on an assault. I already know one of the other dancers is not reporting it, but I am. I didn't say I was positive one of the dancers was a cop. I didn't know her, but I am pretty sure that she was. Not only did she have a uniform, but some of the mayoral security staff knew her personally. I think they called her Patty or something like that."

The officer taking the report stood up and leaned toward her with a pen in her hand, "I'm going to make these copies. I'll be right back."

Tamara was glad that she had brought them with her. In less than a minute the officer was back, "If everything on this report is correct and true, please sign by the "x" and date it and we will get back to you once we have investigated your claims."

"That's it?"

"That's it for now, we'll be in touch." She handed her a generic police department card. "An officer will be assigned to your case and should be in contact with you in the next few days."

She noticed that she dropped the report into the inbox of Joyce C. Rogers as she was escorting Tamara out of the precinct.

Tamara went back home. As she let herself in the front door she noticed another police car driving by her house. She thought; *they never patrolled this neighborhood before. I think Nikki's right. Someone is keeping an eye on us. Cops never patrol this street like this, never.*

She locked her dead-bolt the second she got inside the apartment. Then she called her grandmother as she had promised to do, letting her know that she had made it home all right. After promising her that she would call back again the following day, she hung up the phone. Grabbing the bottle of Vicodin out of her purse she decided that she would take two of them. She didn't take any pain pills before she went downtown to make her police report. She had wanted to have a clear head for that task. Her arm was extremely sore from the activity of driving downtown combined with not taking the medication. She sat in her lazy boy chair and thought about the mayor's wife.

It was understandable her being so pissed off. If the tables were turned and it was her husband with the dancers, she would be pissed too. It actually was one of the reasons she never planned on getting married again. Tamara had zero respect for most men. She had been hit on so many times by married men that she just expected it from them. And the mayor had quite a reputation as a ladies' man. Of course it gave her no right to beat the hell out of us, but never the less, her anger was understandable. Tamara decided not to spend too much time feeling sorry for the mayor's wife, as she could think of a lot of different ways that situation could have been handled. Without the end result getting beat up with a baseball bat. She lived in a mansion, even if she was married to an arrogant jerk. Things could be worse for her. She didn't even have to cook her own food, for crying out loud.

If it didn't hurt so much she would laugh as she thought about the look on the mayors' stunned face. But it did hurt. It hurt that she was the target of his wife's rage. It hurt to know that this was her only way out. That she would have to continue dancing until she finished school because there were no other jobs where she could make a thousand dollars a week. It took a lot of money to support her son and pay for nursing school. Grants and student loans only covered so much. It hurt to think that nothing would be done about the assault. As honestly as she tried to live her life, it didn't matter. She didn't think the police would even question the mayor's wife about the incident. She would bet money on it. They were the pillars of the community and she was "just a stripper".

Her phone rang beside her and jolted her back to reality. She looked at the caller ID.

It was an unknown local number, "Hello?"

A low muffled voice stated, "I think you need to let this drop." Click.

With her heart racing, she set down the phone and went to her closet. Tamara opened the closet door and reached way in the back on the top shelf and pulled out a shoe box. Placing it on the bed she opened it and pulled out a .38 caliber pistol that she kept for protection. She carefully loaded the gun, went back into the living room and set it on the coffee table. She studied the card the officer had given her earlier that day when she had taken her report. The number wasn't the same, but the first six numbers were. 313-220- ****. That call she had just received was from a telephone in the police department. She was almost positive.

She started to be afraid for the first time since all of this started. She double checked her dead-bolt lock, left the living room light on, and carried the gun with her back into the bedroom. She left it on the nightstand where she could reach it with her good arm in case there was an intruder. Once again, she lay in the dark for a long time before sleep claimed her.

Chapter 4.

Someone's Watching

Tamara woke up at 4 A.M. to the sound of her phone ringing. After she glanced at the time and the number, she briefly considered throwing her phone in the toilet. It was her boyfriend Eric.

"Hey sweet thing, I just got back in town, can I come over?"

"Look E, I had a pretty rough weekend and I'm not really in the mood for company right now, I'll call you later." She hung up on him and turned her phone off.

She had told him time and again not to call her in the middle of the night. His head was so far up his own ass that he couldn't get it through to his brain. She was not interested in late night booty calls. He lived in his own world. In his world, a drug dealer was a "pharmaceutical salesperson" and any girl would be honored to have Big "E" as a boyfriend.

Tamara had ignored his advances at the club for more than two years. She had danced for him and taken his money, but never spoke to him outside of the club. She remembered the night that all changed. She had been grabbed rather harshly by her hair and pulled into the lap of a fat man she had been dancing for. A brief shudder claimed her body from head to toe, as she remembered that creep. Scraggly long gray hair, tattered jeans and mean eyes.

She remembered smelling the breath of a thousand drunken bastards as he jerked her forward, pulling her face close to hers and snarled, "You're going home with me tonight."

"The hell I am, let go of my hair! " She yelled, as she tried to pull herself away from him.

The bouncers didn't even have time to react before Eric jumped up from his seat three tables over. He pushed her out of the way and threw the fat slob on the floor. She watched them fight from a safe distance, temporarily forgotten as the men struggled on the dirty concrete floor.

Eric was on top of him, head butting him in his and face asking him, "What part of "don't touch the dancers" don't you understand?"

The bouncers finally made their way over to the fighting men after it was clear they were not going to stop rolling around on the floor any time soon. First they pulled Eric off of him; then they flanked him. Each of them grabbed him by his arms and then they threw him unceremoniously out into the street. He landed on his face and got up sputtering obscenities saying he'd be back. That night Eric walked her out to her car.

She had known that their relationship wasn't anything serious and that it would never end up in marriage. But she wasn't looking for marriage or a serious relationship anyway. He was adult company when she needed some and that was all she had room in her life for. She was trying to raise a man, not find one.

With that thought, she swung back the covers and got out of bed, she wasn't going back to sleep. The digital clock on her bedside table read 4:32 A.M., it wasn't her favorite time to start the day, but she dragged herself into the kitchen and started some coffee anyway. She decided that since she couldn't sleep she would make good use of her time and study, so she pulled out her books. She was so engrossed that several hours had passed and her coffee had gotten cold before she looked up at the clock above the stove with red-rimmed eyes. She couldn't believe it was 8:30 a. m. already. She called Jonathan's dad.

He picked up on the second ring, "Hey Tammy."

" Hi, I was just calling to make sure you got Jonathan to school on time."

"I always get Jonathan to school on time, when there is school. Did you forget its Labor Day? No school today."

"Oh my God, I totally forgot. Is there any way you can keep him a few extra days this week? I have a few things I need to take care of and would really appreciate it."

Adopting a superior tone, he said, "Look Tammy, I told you a million times, I'd keep him here permanently if you'd let him stay. I have no problem taking care of my son."

Tamara wasn't in the mood to deal with it, "Don't start with me, Ernie, I don't need the headache, I just need you to keep him for a few days while I get some things taken care of. I can't talk about it right now; I'll call you in a few days."

The same superior tone came through her line, "Tammy, you better get it together girl. Jonathan comes first."

"You think I don't know that? Give him a kiss for me. I'll call you when I'm ready to pick him up." Then, "Thanks for understanding."

She opened her curtains to let in some sunshine. There was a white SUV parked across the street with someone sitting in it. She wondered if it were an unmarked police vehicle. A similar vehicle had taken her to the hospital the other night. It wasn't until after all that had happened that she had realized those security guards were actually cops that had been assigned to the mayor.

Out loud, to the empty room, she exclaimed, "You have got to be freaking kidding me!" She flipped the vehicle off from her window, not knowing if the driver was looking at her or not and pulled the rod to draw her curtains back together. *It is too beautiful outside to be holed up inside this apartment with the curtains and windows shut.*

She moved her arms over her head and stretched, her arm had started to feel quite a bit better. Tamara decided to go out and meet some friends and get out of the house for the day. She headed to the bathroom to get cleaned up. While she peered into her bathroom mirror, she noticed dark circles under her eyes. She stared back at herself for long seconds and thought that she looked older than her twenty seven years. She reached into the tub and turned on the water as hot as she could stand it and stepped into the shower. Tamara stood under the water long after she had scrubbed herself clean. Half of an hour passed as she stood there. The water finally turned cold and she was forced to get out. It felt so good to be clean. But by the time she had finished dressing her arm was hurting again, throbbing would be a better description.

Lately the Vicodin made her nauseous, so she grabbed a peanut butter sandwich with honey and a glass of milk to wash it down with and went into the living room. She decided to watch some TV and relax until the pill started working. It wasn't long after Tamara consumed her sandwich that it started to kick in.

She pulled a blanket from the back of the sofa over her legs, closed her eyes and laid her head back and dozed off again for an hour or so on the couch. The ringing phone woke her yet again. It was Eric. Once she saw that it was his number, she picked up the phone and apologized immediately. "Hey, E, sorry I hung up on you last night, I was pretty tired, had a rough weekend."

Undaunted, he replied, "So I heard. People talkin' girl."

She rolled her eyes skyward and said, "Yeah, that's all anyone in this town does is talk. Can I crash at your place tonight?"

"Hell musta' froze over. Course you can stay at my place, do you remember where I live?"

Tamara chuckled into the phone, "Just because I don't hang out there don't mean I don't know where it is. I'm going out to a cookout at Belle Isle in a bit. I'll call you when I'm on my way over."

"Awesome babe, I got something for you when you get here."

She laughed, "You always have something for me."

"You'll see, I really got you something. Hit me up when you're on your way."

"M-kay, bye."

He made a kissing noise into the phone and ended the call.

She had rarely stayed over at Eric's house; she wasn't comfortable with all of the foot traffic in and out at all hours of the day and night. When he came over to her house, he put both his phone and pager on vibrate and she could ignore the fact that he sold drugs for a living. Tamara knew that the reason he wanted her to call him when she was en route was so that he could clean out his house for her, the best that he could. All of that aside, she felt better knowing she was going to talk to Eric that night about everything that had been going on and get his advice about it. Eric had a lot of friends and he knew a lot of people. He would probably know more about it than she did. It seemed like he always had the inside scoop about anything going on in this town before anyone else did.

She packed up an overnight bag, double checked that she had turned everything off and headed out the door. As she opened the door she saw that the white SUV was still sitting there across the street. She put her bag in her trunk and decided to drive in that direction to try and get the plate number from the vehicle. She proceeded down the road slowly. When she was almost even with the truck the driver of the vehicle looked directly at her and made his hand in the motion of a gun and mouthed the word, "bang."

Then the driver of the SUV nailed the gas and sped off down the street. There was no way she could see the plate number, it happened way too quickly. She pulled over to the side of the street, shaken from what had just happened. After a minute or so, she pulled herself together enough to continue driving. The driver had on a ski type hat and a hooded sweatshirt pulled up over that, she didn't think she could identify him. The only thing she remembered was his steely-cold eyes and the word *bang*. All she could think was *I'm so screwed. Did that just happen? Someone wants me dead? For what? Filing a police report? This is insane!*

She no longer had a desire to go to the cookout, but she didn't want to go back home either. Her heart was pounding. It took her several long minutes to calm down. Blending into a big crowd seemed like a better idea to her than sitting on the side of the road where her life had just been threatened.

Crossing the MacArthur Bridge onto Belle Isle always made her feel like she was leaving the city behind. It was the largest island city park in the United States. It boasted a half-mile of beach and great views of both Canada and Detroit. It was a popular destination for cook outs, family reunions and graduation parties. Her friends hung out there quite often in the summer time, Labor Day and Memorial Day cookouts were long-standing traditions. With no planning on anyone's part, they all brought meat for the grill, a cooler with whatever they liked to drink and a dish or two to pass. There was never a shortage of good food or drinks. If someone showed up without bringing anything to share, they still left the party with a full belly and yet another great memory of Detroit in the summertime. Tamara had enjoyed Belle Isle with her friends for many years.

Looking down on the island as she crossed over the bridge, she thought, *Belle Isle is kickin'. There ain't no party like a Detroit party.* There were several hundred of people on the island and boats dotted the water from every side of the island. Some of the boats were tied off to each other and the occupants sat in inner-tubes or small rafts and went back and forth taking turns partying on the boat and on the shore. It was a tradition that seemed to get bigger every year. Cars and people were packed in tighter than a busload of people on a tour of celebrity homes in Hollywood. Music was blaring from car stereos and jam boxes and clusters of people were drinking and dancing in small groups. *This is how we do it.* After 15 minutes of driving around slowly; she finally saw her friends. They had lined up several picnic tables. Someone must have gotten there early. Women were sitting around the tables; laughing, talking and setting out food and the men were playing corn-hole and horseshoes while they stood around drinking. A few of her friends waved her in when they saw her car pull up and pointed to a small area between two trucks that she could squeeze her little BMW into. It was a tight fit, but she got it in there on the first try.

When she got out of her car, she popped her trunk open and removed the camp chair and cooler that she had brought. Her old friend walked over to meet her as she joined the group and said," Hey girl, I heard what happened, you ok?"

She noticed that several of her friends were looking at her, waiting for her to answer. "Word sure travels fast around here. I'm alright." She decided to put her chair past the farthest picnic table, in the shade. Tamara removed it from its bag and set it up.

She hoped that her demeanor and the tone she had used would keep anyone else from asking her about it. She kept to herself that day. Part of the crowd, and yet not actively participating in the festivities. What had happened wasn't something she wanted to talk about. She was still trying to process it all. Instead of the sparkling life of the party that she usually was, she sat off to the side and didn't have much to say to anyone. She was distracted by her thoughts and noticed people whispering. She assumed it was about her.

The beer tasted skunk to her, so she dumped it out on the ground and opened another. The second beer tasted off to her too. That's when she realized that it was her, not the beer. The smell of barbeque ribs and burnt hot dogs made her stomach contract. She spent most of the day trying not to vomit while hoping for a good strong wind to blow the aroma of the food in the other direction. She had never felt so alone in her life and looked forward to seeing Eric later that night.

Nakita brought her a bottle of water when she saw that she dumped the second beer out, "That's alcohol abuse, you feeling ok?"

'Yeah, I just don't feel like drinking." She grimaced and took the water, "Thanks."

"Girl, you know this will pass. Next week everybody will be on to the next big rumor. You know how it is."

She had a sinking feeling in her stomach as Nakita said that. She wasn't so sure this would pass in a week. People love drama. It seemed to her like the story was gaining steam like an unstoppable avalanche rather than coming to any kind of a halt. Nakita didn't understand the gravity of her situation, but she *was* being kind. She had started massaging Tamara's shoulders, which felt great.

Looking over her shoulder gratefully, Tamara said, "Thanks, hon. that feels so good." Then she asked her, "Did you finish school yet?"

"I sure did. That is called Myo-therapy; it works great on stress knots. You have a lot of them."

Nakita spent the next thirty minutes talking to Tamara about the spa she had landed a job at. She went on and on about what a bitch the manager was.

At that, Tamara told her, "All managers are bitches: it's a requirement for the job," which made Nakita laugh.

Other than that, she didn't have much to add to the conversation. The chatter was background noise to Tamara. It only required the occasional, *really, no kidding* or *wow.* Thankful for the distraction, she half listened to her old friend as her stomach slowly calmed down. The neck and shoulder massage helped her stress level and it also helped with the headache that had been trying to creep up on her.

Feeling more relaxed; she opened up to her friend, "The cops are watching me. I see them sit outside of my house or drive by. I've been getting threatening phone calls. I don't know what to do. Please don't tell my business to anyone." She spoke in a low tone, not wanting anyone else to hear the conversation.

"You know I don't feed the gossip line, girl. It ain't anybody's business - no way. Maybe you need to lay low and give this all a chance to blow over." Nikita's brow furrowed. She reached out and grabbed both of Tamara's hands and went on to say, "Look, if you need a place to stay, let me know. It might be a good idea to get away for a minute."

Nodding her head in agreement, Tamara replied, "I've been thinking about that. I've been thinking about a lot of things."

"You're a smart girl, Tammy, you'll figure out what to do. You know I'm here."

Tamara stood up, "Thanks, doll, I hope you're right. I'm going over to Eric's to stay tonight."

Nikita hugged her and said, "I love you girl, don't you ever forget it."

"I love you too; it was good seeing you today." One thing about Nakita, she knew how to give a good hug. Her warm hug felt so comforting to Tamara that she almost started to cry, like a small child in her mother's arms. She pulled away, packed her chair up and said her good-bye's to the group as the sun started setting.

It was a short drive to Eric's house, so she decided to call him from her car before she even started it up. He answered on the first ring, "Hey, you home?"

He sounded happy, "Yup. You on your way?"

"Sure am, see you in a few."

She put her car in reverse, *POW, POW, POW*! She about jumped out of her skin. Fucking fireworks! She had to sit there for a minute. *I'm twenty- seven years old and having heart palpitations from fireworks. This whole nightmare has me messed up mentally. I need to get my head together. I can't believe I am getting death threats. It's insane. Why did I ever agree to work the party? I never work parties.*

After a few minutes of focusing on her breathing she was able to calm down enough to concentrate on backing her car out of the tight spot she had parked in. She finally got off Belle Isle and somehow made it to Eric's driveway. She didn't remember making one single turn or stop along the way. She was so preoccupied with her thoughts that the car seemed to drive by itself. She knew she needed to snap out of this daze.

Eric must have seen her pull into the driveway. He came out of his house as she put the car in park. His house was a two story Tudor-style with a porch that ran the length of the house. It had great architecture, but through the years had fallen into a state of disrepair, as had the other houses in the neighborhood. Layers of paint were peeling from the gables and pillars on the outside of the concrete porch. It was a stark contrast from the meticulous way that he maintained the interior. Two security cameras were mounted in the upper corners of the covered porch and pointed to the entrance of the house. She saw Eric's three pit-bulls waiting to greet her by the front door. They looked menacing, but were gentle with Tamara.  They never jumped on her on the few occasions she visited his home.  He had them trained well.

They smiled at each other as he walked toward her car, "Hey, sexy, you look so fine. Pop the trunk and let me get your bag. I've got a surprise for you in the house."

She popped the trunk open for him and said, "E, I don't know if I'm up for anymore surprises right now."

Over his shoulder he promised her, "You'll like this one, I promise." He said as he led the way into his house.

His house was clean, as it always was. Eric was a neat freak. His leather sectional was flanked by glass end tables and a large TV sat in a corner playing hip hop videos on VH1.  A smaller TV on top of it showed a split screen shot of his front and back doors. The familiar scent of Mr. Clean wafted through the house.

Eric set her bag on a chair and went straight into the kitchen, "Come here."

As she entered the tidy kitchen she saw two dozen red roses and a huge bag of Lindorf truffles on the kitchen table.

Opening the bag of truffles was the first thing she did. He knew that was her favorite, "Oh my God, want one?"

Eric laughed and replied, "No, I got 'em for you." He kissed her on the forehead and went back to the stove.

The smell of bacon cooking made her realize she was finally hungry.

"I made some BLT's if you're hungry."

Flashing him a smile she quipped, "I hope you made a lot, I haven't eaten anything today but a peanut butter sandwich. That was hours ago."

"You can eat as much as you want." He placed the last of the bacon on a paper towel, turned off the stove. Then he pulled a plate that had lettuce and tomatoes from the refrigerator. After he put four slices of bread in the toaster, he turned around and hugged her. As he did she winced slightly and pulled back from him.

"My arm's a little sore."

"I heard about everything, we can talk about it all later, after you eat. I'm going to spoil you tonight. I even put fresh sheets on the bed and picked up some bubble bath for you."

As much as she normally didn't like being at his place, that day it seemed comforting. Knowing he had guns in the house would usually keep her away, but not that day. That day she felt safer with her drug dealing boyfriend than she would have felt in the presence of any Detroit cop.

After she had eaten, he ran her a bubble bath, as he had promised. He lit candles that smelled like lilacs and turned off the lights before he brought into the bathroom. He had placed a huge fluffy towel on the toilet, but moved it to the sink, so he could sit in there and talk with her as she took her bath. Once she had finished with her bath, she put on one of his tee shirts and a pair of his boxers. She swam in them, but they were comfortable. He put a Luther Vandross CD in on low and led her by the hand into the bedroom. Eric removed the tee shirt she had just put on, kissed her and turned her around to face the bed. He grabbed his lotion from his dresser and started to massage her gently.

Like most massages go, it turned into sex. Eric was gentle with her. Together, they whispered long into the night. Eric reiterated what Nikita had said. He told her it might not be a bad idea for her to lay low for a while. He told her that she was being watched. It wasn't her imagination. He had been paying off certain officers for many years - it was the cost of doing business in this town. He had received more than one call about this deal. That's what he paid them for, timely heads up. Certain individuals were displeased that she had made a police report. The word on the street was that they were keeping a close eye on her.

She listened to him carefully and understood what he was saying, but told him, "Look, E, I have a kid. I can't just drop my life and disappear. He has school, I have school."

"School ain't going anywhere. That school will be there when things cool down. The kid needs to be safe; you should think about letting him stay with Ernie, just until this blows over. You can't let him get mixed up in the middle of this."

Tears were in her eyes as she looked at him and said, "He wouldn't understand."

Eric had a compassionate look on his face as he told her, "Sometimes you have to do what you have to do. Think about what I said. I have a place you can go if you need a place. "

The tears spilled onto her cheeks, "I appreciate that Eric, but I have a place to go if I need to. It just isn't fair. None of this is fair."

He held her close and whispered, "Things have a way of working out. You need to get some rest. I'm not going to let anything happen to you here."

His arms felt safe around her. She lay still, feigning sleep as she thought long into the night about the things he had said.

The next morning she woke up with the sunlight streaming on her face and it took her a couple of minutes to acclimate herself. The smell of fresh coffee wafted down the hall mixed with the acrid aroma of high grade marijuana.

She walked into his kitchen to get a cup of coffee. She glanced up by the door where he was speaking in low tones to someone. His company appeared to be just leaving.

She over heard him say, "Tell Rico I said no more fronts, I'm not a bank and I don't make loans. I want my money Friday."

"Ok, boss." Then the door shut with a click. She watched his guest leave the property on the surveillance TV. He got into a Mustang with tinted windows. Eric's surveillance cameras had four screens in one and she found it interesting to watch.

He turned around and saw her standing there, "How did you sleep? I didn't wake you up, did I?"

Tamara smiled at him, "I slept great, for a change."

"Want to wake and bake?" He pointed to the half joint that was still smoldering in the ashtray on the table.

Shaking her head, "No, thanks, you know I don't do that shit."

He smiled and walked over to give her a hug. "You sure are looking beautiful this morning. What you doing today?"

She ignored his questions as she started gathering her things. His phone and pager were both vibrating on the coffee table every few seconds.

Tamara put her make-up bag in her overnight bag, "I can't stick around; I'll probably try to get back to work by the end of the week. My arm is healing fast and I need the cash. Let me know if you hear anything else."

"You got it babe, just get on with things the best you can until this whole thing blows over. If things get worse, remember what we talked about. Girl, you know I love you."

"I know you do. I appreciate you more than you think. I'll call you later."

After she put her shoes on she grabbed her bag and kissed him. She was ready to go. He tried to turn it into more than a goodbye kiss, grabbing her butt and pushing her back toward the bedroom. Some things never change. Tamara pulled away and told him she would see him soon. They were both smiling as she walked out the door.

Chapter 5.

Divine Assistance Please

She decided she needed help with her situation, help that Eric couldn't provide, divine help. It had been a long time, but she punched the number of Grace Bible Church into her phone before she backed out of Eric's driveway. Reverend Ken Hampton answered after a few rings.

"Reverend, this is Tamara Greene."

"Tamara dear, it's been far too long since we have seen you. Since when did you stop calling me dad?" He said jovially, his voice conveying that was genuinely happy to hear from her.

She had been calling him dad for years. He knew that she didn't have a father from the counseling he had with her, before her baptism. He had told her then, that he would be a dad to her whenever she needed one. He was a wonderful man and Tamara loved him dearly.

His words brought tears to her eyes instantly. "It has been too long. Is there any way you can meet with me today? I have something I really need to talk to you about. It's important."

Concern crept into his voice, "Yes, of course. Can you meet me at the Gospel House Bible Book Store at 11?

Relieved that he had the time to meet her that same day, she let out a long breath of air before replying, "That sounds perfect, I'll see you then."

She had two hours to kill before she was to meet with her pastor. She headed home. The white SUV sitting down the street from her apartment was no surprise to her by this time. Shivering, despite the warm day, she hit the button on her key fob twice to double check that the car had locked. Hearing the comforting beep from behind her, she let herself into her apartment. After clicking the deadbolt into place, she dropped her things on the sofa and went straight into the shower. When she finished showering; she deliberated for a half hour about what to wear. Half a dozen outfits were tossed on the bed and around the room until she finally decided to wear a hot pink

jogging suit.

Wasting no time hanging around her apartment she gathered

her things and headed out.    While she drove to meet the

Reverend she indulged herself by pressing the one button on her

stereo that played the classic rock station WRIF. Pink Floyd,

*"Wish You Were Here"* was playing and she cranked the Bose

speakers up as high as she could and sang with the band,

*"So, so you think you can tell; heaven from hell, blue skies from pain?*
*Can you tell a green field, from a cold steel rail?*
*A smile through a veil, do you think you can tell?*
*Did they get you to trade, your hero's for ghosts?*
*Hot ashes for trees?  Hot air for a cool breeze? Cold comfort for change?*
*Did you exchange, a walk on part in a war, for a lead role in a cage?"*

The song ended as she pulled into the parking lot. Tamara had

arrived at the book store ten minutes early and browsed the

shelves a bit as she waited for the Reverend. Her eyes were

drawn to "The Purpose Driven Life." It had a huge display in the

middle of the store with hundreds of copies on it.  She picked up a copy and thumbed through it, the reviews were good, but money was tight, so she decided not to buy it. She sat down in a chair and waited for the Reverend to arrive.

It wasn't long before she saw him walk through the door. He saw her wave to him and made his way over to where she was sitting, "Tammy, dear, it's been too long."

"I know, dad." She looked down at the floor, "You've probably heard what I've been doing."

Reverend Hampton replied, "Yes, I've heard what you've been doing. I've not been pleased with what I've heard."

"I know, I know, it's only till I finish school." Then she said, "Dad, I have a big problem. Some people are out to get me."

Surprise registered on his face, "Who's out to get you sweetheart? What are you talking about?

Shaking his head, she told him; "It's not something I can talk about"

His forehead furrowed into many lines as he asked her yet another question, "What do you mean when you say they're out to get you? Is someone threatening you?"

She looked at him earnestly, "Yes, I am being followed and threatened. I can't really talk about it, but I need you to pray for me. My life may be in danger. I can't elaborate, these are powerful people."

The reverend looked visibly saddened by what he had heard. His brow was furrowed again as he reached for both of the hands of the girl that he had known for so long.

He said to her lovingly, "There is nothing too big for our God, and you belong to Him. I don't know what is going on in your life right now Tammy, but He does. Let's take this to Him."

They bowed their heads close together, held hands and the Reverend prayed, "Dear holy heavenly Father, I don't know what your precious child Tamara is going through right now. But I know that you do. I pray that you would keep her safe from all harm. Protect her under the shadow of your wings. I thank you for Tamara, Lord, and the joy that she brings into our lives. I pray that you would break into pieces any weapon formed against her, Lord. Let her feel your loving arms around her as you lead her and give her direction. This is your child, Lord. I pray the blood of Jesus cover her and keep her safe. Set your angels around her, Lord. Protect her family, protect her home and always let her know how very much you love her, Lord. Bless her now and always. It's in Jesus precious name that we pray, Amen."

"Amen. " Tamara said, and then she looked up into his kind face. Her eyes were two oceans at full tide as she fought desperately to hold back her tears. For what seemed like the millionth time since the party.

He spoke kindly; "I hope you know we love you."

And for the millionth time the tears spilled onto her cheeks, "I know Dad, thanks."

The reverend reached into his pocket and pulled out a folded linen hanker-chief and handed it to her, "You know, we would love to see you in church Sunday."

Tamara wiped her eyes, "I know. My work schedule makes it hard."

The Reverend sighed, "Are you still going to nursing school?"

She handed him back his used hanky; "Yes, but I only have one class this semester."

He placed his hand on her shoulder and told her; "You are going to be a wonderful nurse, Tammy, the best."

Tamara smiled up into his kind face, "Thanks Dad, I really appreciate you meeting me today. Please keep praying for me, I'm running low on places to turn."

"You bet I will, sweetheart." They rose to their feet and he pulled her close in a hug that lasted long seconds.

"Come on, honey, I'll walk you out."

He held the door open for her. The fall air had turned sharply colder. Michigan weather was so unpredictable. The cold air blasted them in the face as they walked against the wind into the parking lot where they both had parked.

He escorted her to her car, "Please take care, dear, and I hope we see you in church real soon."

She reached up to give him a final hug before she opened the door and slid into the seat "I love you, Dad. Thanks for everything."

"Any time, sweetheart, any time."

He started toward his car, stopped, turned around and watched her as she pulled away from the lot. He whispered another prayer for her under his breath before he turned away with a long sigh.

Chapter 6.

The Store

While the visit with the Reverend had made her feel better, it proved to be only temporary. This feeling she had of being watched and the threats hanging over her head made her a wreck. She had several calls a day from unavailable numbers where a person was just on the other end of the phone line, breathing. She had no sooner turned her car into her driveway when she received another such one of those calls.

"Who are you? Leave me alone!" She screamed into the phone before throwing it against the dash of her car.

She immediately rescued her phone from the floor where it had landed and made sure that it was still in working order. She thought, *That's it, I'm out of here!* Tamara threw her phone into her purse, snatched her keys from the ignition and went in the house.

She dug out several bags for herself and two suitcases for Jonathan. There was no way she was going to bring her son home to this. He would have to stay with his dad until this crap was over. Tamara packed her car up with enough clothes and the personal items that she thought would see them both through a few weeks. Then she headed over to Ernie's house to talk to him and Jonathan.

Ernie lived out in the suburbs of the city. It was a fifteen minute drive, but she deliberately drove a few suburbs past his when she exited the highway. She didn't want those pricks knowing where her son was. Once she was sure she had not been followed, she circled back around and pulled her car onto Outer Drive and headed in the right direction. It didn't take her long; she was on his tree lined street and up into his driveway at the end of the cul-de-sac within minutes.

The talk with Ernie was the easy part. He loved having Jonathan there with him. He always made it crystal clear that he would be more than happy to keep Jonathan full-time. There was never an instant in time that she didn't know that.

The talk with her son was a bit more difficult. "I don't want to stay with dad, mom. I want to go home with you."

She tried to explain, "I can't go home right now either. This will just be for a few weeks son."

He was visibly upset, his voice raised a pitch; "Why can't we go home? I want to go home."

Her eyes begged him to understand. She told him, "There are some things in life that you won't understand until you're grown up. This is one of them."

Jonathan pleaded with her, "I'm smarter than you think I am, mom. Tell me. Why I can't go home."

Tamara reached out and gently pulled his face away from the window, toward her; "Jonathan, look at me. I love you; nothing will ever change that. I'm sorry that this is the way it has to be right now. I promise you; I'll explain all of this to you when you're a little older. I promise." Her eyes once again pleaded with him to understand, it was a lot to ask for from a thirteen year old child.

"Ok, mom, please don't cry. I love you, mom." He wrapped his arms around her and hugged her so tight that she had a hard time catching her breath. She hugged him back almost as hard, and thought; *I am the luckiest woman in the world to have you for my son. There is nothing I wouldn't do for you, nothing.*

She held him tightly and told him, "I love you too, son. More than you will ever know. I'll call you every day after you get home from school. It won't be for long son. I'll get this straightened out, I promise."

He pulled back and weakly smiled at her, "I know you will mom, you're the smartest lady I know."

She smiled back gratefully, "I have to get going now. I'll call you tomorrow. Be good for your dad."

His smile didn't reach his sad eyes; "Ok mom, love you."

Getting into her car, she turned back to him and softly said, "Love you more," Then she slid into the car with a sigh, closed the door and backed the car out of the driveway. When she looked down at her phone she saw that she had three missed calls from unknown numbers. After some self deliberation as she drove, she decided that she would stay a few nights at Nikki's.

Nikki spent that week packing her things. She had decided to move back to Atlanta. Tamara could tell by her tone that she wasn't happy with her.

"I've been getting phone calls telling me your friend better back off. I told you no good would come from making that police report. I ain't even did nothing and they won't stop calling my phone."

Tamara packed bath towels from Nikki's linen closet into a box, "So that's it, you're just going to run away and pretend it never happened?"

Nikki had decided she was moving back to Atlanta.

"I don't need this shit."

"What about Darrell?" Tamara was referring to Nikki's boyfriend.

"What about him? He's a bigger chicken-shit than I am."

Tamara laughed at that, "I guess what you do is your business. I'm not staying at my house right now either, but I did make a report. No one has the right to lay their hands on me. I swore to myself a long time ago that I wouldn't put up with being hit by anyone, ever again, as long as I live. I can't break that promise to myself. I won't"

Nikki finished taping a box shut. She reached on the counter for her pack of Newport cigarettes and sat down at the table with a long sigh.

She pulled one out of the pack and lit the tip with a green bic lighter. Nikki drew the smoke deep into her lungs before answering Tamara, "I hear ya girl.. I understand what you're saying. But this here ain't nothin' but trouble. This is the mayor's wife. Think about the phone calls you been getting and that car sitting down the street right now. It ain't worth it, girl."

No matter how hard she tried that day, Tamara never was able to get her friend to understand why it mattered to her. Why she had to make the report. By the end of that week Nikki had left the state.

After Nikki had moved, Tamara started staying over at Eric's house. She parked her car in his neighbor's garage. Eric worked that out with the neighbor; he thought it was best for her not to park openly in his driveway. By the end of that week Tamara felt well enough to go back to work.

Jerry acted very curt with her the minute she walked in the door, "You're late."

She had just walked in the door, her eyes had not fully acclimated to the dark club and already he was on her? "Whatever, Jerry." She knew how much money she made him. *Besides, it was three minutes!*

She walked into the shabby dressing room. It had high school gym style lockers and mirrors with large spider-web cracks from where someone had been screwing or fighting and slammed it. It smelled like a gym, sweat and funky body odor. A thin veneer of cheap perfume didn't quite mask the odor. She popped two Vicodin and chased them down with a nice warm drink of Grand Marnier to get through the shift, pulled out her gear and transformed herself into Strawberry. In her thigh-high boots, latex shorts, halter top and wig, she hardly recognized herself in the dirty mirror. She got ready for work, applying false eyelashes with a steady hand. Deciding on one last dash of lip gloss, she put it on and threw her things back into her bags. She set her next outfit on top of the bags and locked up her belongings. Concentrating on getting ready for work helped her not to think about everything that had happened lately.

Strawberry was surprised to hear grunge rock blaring from the speakers as she made her way back into the club area. Occasionally when powerful or famous people came in, Jerry would play whatever kind of music they liked. It was a Temple of the Dog tune, Hunger Strike, blasting through the sub-woofers in the dank, half-empty club.

*I don't mind stealing bread……… from the mouths of decadence*
*But I can't feed on the powerless……… when my cup's already*
*overfilled*

Strawberry looked around the club and noticed that some familiar faces from the mayoral party were there, the same assholes that escorted her to the hospital with a few new faces besides. Her heart raced as the music got progressively louder with the tempo of the song,

*Blood is on the table, the fire is cook-iiiiiiiiiiiiinnnnnn'*
*But I'm going hungry (going hungry)*
*I'm going hungry (Going hungry)*

Her stomach clenched when she realized that she had a police escort even while she was working and there was nothing she could do about it. *No wonder Jerry was such a jerk. It couldn't be good for business to have cops crawling all over the club. Uniform or not, anyone breathing on Eight Mile could spot a cop a mile away.*

As she walked over to where Jerry was perched in his striped button-down bowling shirt, she noticed that he looked a little nervous and none too happy. She spoke to him in a low tone leaning in close to him as if she were going to kiss his cheek, "So, Jerry, how long has this been going on or just tonight?"

He turned his head slightly, cut his eyes at her and said, "Been waiting for ya' all week, baby girl, all week long."

Her eyebrows were raised as she shrugged slightly and sarcastically asked him; "I'm guessing they like grunge rock?" Then more seriously; "Look Jerry, I can't do this anymore."

Jerry leaned in closer to her ear again; "I've got eyes and ears girl, I can only guess what you're dealing with. We'll miss you."

They way he looked at her when he said that conveyed his sadness. The finality of his statement was palatable. She knew that her job there had come to an end.

Strawberry noticed that two of the un-uniformed officers were leaning on their chairs, straining to listen in on their conversation. It was almost laughable how obvious they were, almost. *What the hell can I do? While they weren't very good at being inconspicuous, they were masters at intimidation, I ain't got any respect for any man threatening or scaring a girl. Prick cops. Are there no crimes in this city to solve? I'm not only on the run, now I have no frickin' job.*

Strawberry stood there for long seconds before she replied to what Jerry had said. Then she looked him straight in the eye and said loudly, "Screw you, you fat son of a bitch. I quit." She picked up his drink sitting on the bar and threw it in his face for good measure. *Actually, that part felt pretty damn good. I could have been one hell of an actress.*

Unable to stop herself when she saw the surprise and shock on his face, she threw her head back and laughed so hard she almost pissed herself.

His face was instantly red, he drew back his arm as if to slap her, changed his mind, pointed at the door and yelled, "You better get out of here while you still can."

She slung her head to the side, pivoted on her heels and swished her ass with an exaggerated sway off the club floor. She knew she wouldn't be coming back, so she made sure to do a once over in the locker room making sure all of her belongings were in her bag. In the background she heard Pearl Jam pumping through the club, 'I'm Still Alive'

*"Is something wrong? She said - of course there is.*
*You're still alive. She said - oh do I deserve to be?*
*Is that the question? And if so, if so, who answers, who answers?*

She felt bad for those poor girls that had to try to dance to that music. She left the club and drove around for hours. Even Eric didn't want her car to be seen at his house. So many things flooded through her mind as she drove mindlessly. Hours passed by as the night sky into the first morning light. She stayed in the outlying suburbs of Detroit until the sun shone high in the sky.

Eric must have wondered why she didn't stay at his house. He had called her three times and left messages. When she had left the club, she had turned her phone off; she just wanted some time to herself to think about things. His last message indicated that he wanted her to come over to his house the minute she got his message. His message said, "Just come no matter what time it is."

It was 8 A.M., which Tamara knew was early for Eric. She turned the stereo off as she pulled into his driveway. She could hear his dogs barking as she walked up his steps. He must've been awake, because he answered his door right away, "Hey baby, come in."

"I didn't think you'd be up. You're not going to believe this. I quit my job at All Stars last night."

Eric shook his head and smiled, "Girl, you know I done heard about that. You quitting Tiger Club too?"

"I don't know, I'm thinking about taking off for a while."

He had the biggest grin on his face, "You might want to think twice about that. I have something for you."

"What you talking about?"

He grabbed her hand and pulled her into the kitchen and sat her down in a chair, "Close your eyes."

"Come on Eric, what is it?"

He reached into a kitchen drawer and pulled out a thick envelope and handed it to her. She opened it. It was full of one hundred dollar bills. "Eric, what is this? Where did this come from?"

"It's for you. It's thirty grand."

Her eyes were wide and incredulous, "You're kidding me, right?"

"I'm not kidding. You don't have to dance if you don't want to, girl. I want to talk to you about opening a lingerie store."

She kept repeating his words back to him, "A lingerie store? I'm going to nursing school."

He looked at her, "You can make more money with the store. You know a lot of dancers. You can cater to them and make a killing."

Tamara looked at the money, then back up to Eric, "What about the cops? I can't do anything Eric. I'm ready to hit the road."

"If you open this store and mind your own business, no one is going to be bothering you anymore."

She knew Eric had informants, but this was a lot to take in. Where did this money come from? She knew Eric always had a wad of cash. But this was a lot of money.

"You're sure about that?"

"I'm sure. C'mon, let's go for a ride. I want to show you some places for lease. Let's go find you a store."

Tamara started laughing and spoke in circles, "Eric, I've been up all night! I can't believe this. Are you sure? There's no way I could sleep right now anyway – let's go."

Within a few days, they had found a building on the west-side of Detroit. She had decided to name her store, 'Tammy's Secrets'. After a week had gone by with no one following her or calling her and hanging up, she thought it would be okay to bring Jonathan back home. It had seemed as if things were back to normal, whatever normal was.

Jerry had called her and asked her to come back to work, so she did, for one night a week. She was surprised that he had called her back, after the drink incident. Jerry knew she had a lot of regulars; it was either - call her back to work, or lose his clients to the Tiger Club. She stayed on at both clubs - one night a week. It was enough to pay the bills while she worked getting the store ready. It also maintained a network of entertainers for her to sell merchandise to when her store opened.

Her days were spent ordering beach-wear and lingerie from California, and stocking the shelves with eye-catching displays.

She loved the store and worked hard to get it ready. Tamara was planning to open the boutique May 1, 2003. The days on the calendar flew by as she readied the store.

It was finally the week of her opening. She was so busy that she had forgotten to ask for the week off from the clubs. Tuesday she had to work at All Stars and Saturday at the Tiger Club. It was going to be a hectic week. Some of the merchandise that she ordered would be late arriving. She was out of money. Tamara had told Eric last week that she was going to need more cash to get everything up and running. Her head was full of details about her store.

She wasn't tired Tuesday night, after working at the club. She called Eric to see if he was still awake. He answered on the third ring, "Hey, doll."

"Hey Eric, you up?"

He didn't sound sleepy, although it was almost 3 A.M. "Yeah, swing by."

"I can't stay. If I swing by can you come outside? I want to ask you something about the store."

"Sure thing, babe, I'm waiting on someone anyway."

Tamara pulled into his driveway, as she told him on the phone, "I'm here."

He came out smiling, with some swagger in his step, he always seemed so happy to see her. And he really did have a nice smile. He proved himself to be a good friend through all of this. She knew that he loved her.

He got into the car and said, "Hey, do you mind pulling over on the curb and waiting for a minute? I'm waiting on someone."

Tamara tossed him an appreciative glance; "After everything you've done for me? You got it."

She backed her car onto the street and then pulled over to the curb by where he pointed and put it in park. She didn't bother to turn the car off.

They made small talk as they waited on his friend. She started telling him about the merchandise that was going to be delivered late, and all of the details yet to finish before the big grand opening. They were both looking up the street when they saw a white SUV turn the corner. It slowed down as it got closer to them.

Tamara looked at Eric, "You friggin' have to be kidding me?"

What she saw in his face frightened her - he had a trapped look on his face and fear in his eyes. Her heart beat like thunder in her ears as she turned back away from Eric to see the SUV almost even with the car.

The SUV slowed down as it pulled up parallel to where she was parked and in slow motion she watched the tinted glass roll down. The black barrel of a gun was all she saw as her ears started to roar, she couldn't move as much as an eyelash.

Eric crouched down into the seat, pulling her arm with him, and screamed, "Get down! Get down!"

Recognition crossed her face and then not even seconds later, before she could think or react to what was happening, bullets riddled through her body. *Jesus, help me, Jesus,* would be her final thoughts. And just that quickly, her life here was over as her blood spilled out into the car that fateful morning.

Eric had been hit too. He saw all of the blood and shouted, "Tammy, Tammy!"

Once he realized that she was dead, he crawled out of the car and loped his way to the nearest house. He pounded on the door, begging for entry. They wouldn't open the door, so he yelled, "Call 911. I'm shot, my girlfriend's been shot. Call 911." Then he collapsed on their porch and waited for help.

Chapter 7.

Reverend Hampton

The Reverend heard about her death on the evening news. After he watched it on several stations, he shut the door to his office and wept for Tamara. He remembered how young and scared she looked last fall, in her pink outfit, as she asked him for prayer. When he hadn't heard anything from her after that day, he had assumed that everything had been worked out. Such a shame, at twenty-seven years old, he still considered her a kid.

With the media going bananas with claims and inquiries about her dancing at the Manoogian Mansion and some altercation with the mayor's wife, things started to make a bit of sense. It was a sad situation. He hoped there was no such connection, but it did make sense.

He prepared for the sermon that he would give at her funeral in a few short days and thought about the way her smile could light up a room. What a joy she was, with her bubbly personality and her love of life. Tamara was such a dear girl. He knew that she would be missed by so many.

The day of her funeral came and the church was bursting at the seams with huge flower arrangements and throngs of people. Her family was all seated in the front rows. Many of them had driven in from other states. He had met with them earlier when he offered prayer and his condolences. There had to be over four hundred people in attendance. Some people were standing in the back because there was not enough room in the church for everyone to sit down.

After he opened the service with a word of prayer, Tamara's young niece sang "Amazing Grace." By the time she got to the final verse:

*When we've been there, ten thousand years, bright shining as the sun*
*We've no less grace to sing God's praise, then when we first begun.*

There was not a dry eye in the church, her clear voice rang out in perfect harmony with the piano and it sounded as if it were sung by an angel. The Reverend had to clear his throat to regain his composure before he could speak and share with them a portion from the word of God.

He wasn't surprised that Tamara had so many loved ones. She was a special girl. After he finished both the service at the church and the short one at the gravesite he went back to the luncheon and sat down with a plate of food by Tamara's grandmother, Christine White.

He sat beside her and offered to her his condolences, "I'm very sorry that you've lost your granddaughter."

Looking at him through swollen eyelids she replied, "Thank you, Reverend. You did a good job with the service."

He leaned in closer toward her, "You know I spoke with Tamara a few months ago. She told me that she was afraid of someone, but she never told me who it was."

She cast a quick look behind her, then leaned in toward him and said, "She told me the same thing. She told me she did dance at that party, you know. I think that's why she was scared, can I tell you something?"

"Of course you can."

"Tammy was afraid of the police. I done had at least twenty people tell me there was a bunch of cops at the funeral today." She looked behind her once again; making sure no one was listening in on their conversation.

He didn't touch his food as they talked. "I also have been hearing the same thing. I have a video tape of the funeral. I'm going to make a copy of it and give it to Detroit Homicide. Maybe it can help them with their investigation."

She had a skeptical look on her face, "It can't hurt. Tammy was a good girl, you know. She wouldn't hurt a flea. Only reason she danced was to go to school and make a better life for the boy."

He placed his hand over her wrinkled hand on the table, assuring her, "I knew her well, Ms. White. Tammy was a wonderful girl. She will be missed"

The hurt look on her face prompted him to change the subject, he asked her, "When are leaving to go back home?"

"Tuesday morning. We're driving home; we should be home by Wednesday night. We usually stay a night in Tennessee when we make the trip so it isn't so hard on us."

He reached in his pocket and pulled out one of his cards and handed it to her, "That makes sense, it's a long drive. I hope you know that you can call me if you ever need to talk."

She slid it into her wallet immediately, "Thank you for everything Reverend. I can see why Tammy liked coming here to this church. It's so beautiful and you are such a nice man."

After covering his uneaten food with a crumpled napkin, he stood to his feet and told her, "Thank you, I'm going to be leaving now. I hope you have a safe trip home."

Ms. White patted his hand, "Thanks Reverend."

He no sooner than stood up and another family member took his seat to spend a few minutes visiting with her. After another half hour of goodbyes he made his way out of the door. A headache was starting in his temple and he was glad he left when he did. It was a long week. Tamara was very dear to him and his job was a tough one sometimes. He was comforting others when he needed comfort himself. The situation was troubling to him.

He spent the following day in his office making several copies of Tamara's funeral service. The family wanted two copies of it; he made one to take to the police department and another two in case he had another order. One of them he placed in his safe. There was too much talk about police officers being at her funeral. He had spent many years as a police officer himself before he became a minister.

On May 9th, 2003, he took a copy of the funeral video and headed downtown. After circling around a parking structure for fifteen minutes he found a spot to park and walked into Detroit Police Department for the first time in a long time. He was instructed to have a seat while they figured out which squad in homicide was handling the Tamara Greene case. Looking around, he noticed that not all that much had changed. Twenty minutes later Lieutenant Jackson came out to where he was seated and introduced himself.

Firmly shaking his hand he said, "Nice to meet you Reverend, would you like to come back to my office where we can talk."

Standing to his feet, he replied, "That'll be great, I won't take up much of your time."

As Jackson led the way up to the third floor, down several hallways and into an office that had his name and title on the door, he explained, "Marian Stevenson is the Officer in Charge of the case, she is one of our top Detectives, and she is out taking statements this afternoon. I can take whatever information you have for her and make sure that she gets it."

Jackson sat down behind his desk and gestured to the other chair, "Please, have a seat." He moved an empty red-stained Tupperware dish from the center of his desk. Pulled out a yellow legal-pad and a pen and sat it on the desk.

The Reverend sat down and cleared his throat, "Tamara had called me a few months ago and asked me to meet with her. I met with her at a bookstore and she told me that she was afraid and that someone was "out to get her." I tried to get her to tell me who it was, but she wouldn't elaborate. I talked to her grandmother at her funeral and she told me that she had a similar conversation with Tamara. "

Jackson was rapidly taking notes as he spoke, "Go on."

"She told me that Tamara had called her and told her that she had danced at the Manoogian mansion and that she had an altercation with the mayor's wife. She also told me that Tamara had been scared since that day and that she was afraid of the police. I'm not sure how she knew police officers, but several people told me that there were a lot of Detroit cops present at the funeral. I thought if you guys had the video it might help you with the case."

Jackson looked up from the notes he had been writing, "I appreciate you coming forward with this information. Stevenson will be back later on this afternoon. I'll make sure she gets this right information away."

The Reverend stood to his feet, "Thank you for your time. Please leave my card and this letter for Ms. Stevenson. If I can be of any further assistance, I will be happy to help any way I can. She was a nice girl, you know."

Jackson stood and shook the Reverends hand, "I'm sure she was; we'll do everything we can to find her killer, sir."

"That's all anyone can expect."

Jackson held the door open for the Reverend, "Can you find your way back out?"

He smiled, "Yes, I used to work here. Thanks."

Reverend Ken Hampton walked out feeling better than he had in days. His gut told him that Jackson was a good man. If anyone could get to the bottom of this and find out who killed Tamara, he could. He made it a point not to watch the local news for a few weeks. All of the reporting on Tamara's murder and the constant allegations about the mayor and his staff was disturbing for him to see. He needed to be full of hope. His ministry required it. He included Tamara's family in his nightly prayers for many months.

Chapter 8.

Gary Brown

Gary Brown had been a Detroit Police Officer for over 26 years and in the last year of his employment he was proud to work under Jerry Oliver, Chief of Police, as the head of Internal Affairs. Upon his placement in the position, he promptly changed the name of the department to Professional Accountability Bureau. His task was to raise the level of professionalism in the police department, and all other city employees. Approximately 14,000 city employees fell under his purview, from the mayor to the street sweeper. He had worked hard to get where he was and his strong ethics pushed him to not only run his department smoothly and efficiently, but also to study models at the Justice Department in Washington D. C. and re-write departmental policies and procedures. They had to be approved by a committee, but he personally was re-writing the entire manual.

March 28th started as any other day, a morning meeting consisting of dispatching teams of investigators, updating himself on ongoing cases and reviewing information that concluded cases. He never realized that morning when he sent Officers McClure and Lawrence out to take a report from Harold Nelthrope that he would be setting in motion the end of his own career.

All of his officers knew that if it was a case or report of a highly sensitive nature, or if it had the potential of becoming newsworthy, they were to phone him at home any hour of the day or night. It was very seldom he had any such calls, but it was important for a man in his position to be available around the clock.

His phone rang around 8 P.M.; it was McClure, "Brown here."

"Our visit to Nelthrope today brought some rather interesting allegations to light."

"Such as?"

"First of all, when we arrived at his home, he said he had already received a threatening phone call warning him to back off of the EPU and keep his mouth shut. He insisted on meeting in his home and he was wearing a bullet proof vest."

Gary Brown listened intently; "That's interesting. Go on."

McClure continued, "He alleges that he was transferred a few months ago to the 7th precinct after questioning overtime worked by members of the executive protection unit. He also alleges that certain members of the Executive Protection Unit were in accidents that involved the use of city vehicles. Also alleges that EPU employees were drinking and driving while on duty"

Gary interjected with a question, "Were any accidents involving city vehicles reported?"

"Not to my knowledge."

He asked McClure another question, "Who was named in the complaint?"

"Both Officer Martin and Officer Jones from the EPU were named."

He advised him; "Well, document everything in writing and have a report on my desk first thing Monday morning. Pull Martin and Jones phone records so I can review them and determine if either one of them called Nelthrope or had any incoming calls from our office between the time I assigned you to take the complaint and the time the visit was made to his home"

"Will do."

Appreciative for the heads up, Brown said, "Thanks for the call, have a good weekend."

"You too."

The following Monday came and went without a report from McClure gracing his desk. It was not the first time McClure failed to follow through on a direct order. That was grounds for immediate termination and was not something he tolerated from his subordinates.

Wednesday, he called McClure into his office," Where is the report from Nelthrope that I asked you for on Monday?"

McClure looked at an invisible spot his computer screen and said, "I haven't had the time to type it up."

Gary Brown was not tolerant of insubordination, "I suggest you make the time if you like working in this department. Get it done and on my desk."

Considering the positions they both held, trust and integrity had to be the core principals displayed at all times and in every situation. Transparency of each action taken, as it related to investigations of other officers, was an imperative trait for all members of his department. It had to be apparent in all that were assigned to his team for Brown to have an effective presence on the police force.

There were so many cases that Gary was working on, serious breaches in professionalism and ethical conduct within the Detroit Police Department. Money confiscated from drug busts that was missing from evidence, non-compliance with standard protocols and outright criminal activity from law enforcement officials. Corruption was rampant. He took the job of cleaning the police department up seriously. That's what Jerry Oliver had hired him to do. Trust within his department was not just a word on some wish list; it was something that had to exist.

By Friday, Gary still did not have his report. He stormed in McClure's office without knocking, "You can go ahead and box your stuff up. You are being transferred to the first precinct."

McClure never looked up from his desk. He said flatly, "Sure thing."

Gary was unimpressed and had McClure's phone records pulled to review later that day. As well as certain members that he asked for from the EPU. He spent the rest of the afternoon reviewing phone records with his neon-green highlighter in his hand. He was good at his job. Before the day ended he walked into Lawrence's office and sat down unceremoniously.

"McClure has been transferred to the first precinct. If I don't have that memo regarding Nelthrope's complaint on my desk within two days, you may be joining him. If you need a second interview, go back out there, but get that report on my desk ASAP."

Lawrence looked up at him and said, "I do need a second interview, McClure didn't write out the complete list of the allegations and I need that information if we are going to investigate the claims fully."

"Make it a priority and get me something in writing. I don't need to tell you that this could be explosive. I want this handled right."

Gary understood and expected as much. He was not pleased when anyone on his staff didn't follow his orders, especially as it related to something of such a sensitive nature. Uncovering the layers to investigate misdeeds of police officers on a good day was not an easy task. With members of the EPU involved. It seemed to Brown like a tooth extraction with a pair of rusty pliers and no Novocain; would have been easier.

The report from Lawrence appeared on his desk by the middle of the following week. Seeing as Nelthrope had worked in EPU for some length of time, his direct knowledge of the allegations was very probable. While he could be disgruntled about his involuntary transfer out of EPU, his allegations were serious and required further inquiry.

He took the report to Brian Stair, who was at the time in charge of the public corruption unit, better known as PCU. Within two weeks Brian had done extensive footwork on the case and arranged to meet to discuss his findings.

Gary sat down in the stained chair that was across from his desk, "Looks like Nelthrope's claims have some merit."

Gary looked at him intently and asked, "Which claims? The excessive overtime or the accidents?"

"Both. There were EPU vehicles that were badly damaged. The vehicles were sent back to the dealership due to the extent of the damage. Also, the reports that excessive overtime had been worked seemed to check out too. Some of the officers on a $49,000 a year salary made over $110,000."

Gary interrupted him with a question, "Did Nelthrope personally witness any of this?"

Stair answered him; "No, it's all third party information. But he did say he kept a diary during his time at EPU."

"He kept a diary?"

Stair hesitated for a second; then he went on to say, "He said he did. On my second visit with him, he brought up another claim about some parties at the Manoogian Mansion. One in particular in the fall of 2002, women were dancing naked and the mayor's wife arrived home unexpectedly and assaulted the dancers. He also alleged that the dancers required medical treatment."

Gary Brown rubbed his chin thoughtfully; "Due to HIPPA laws, we can't get hospital records."

Stair assured him, "I can investigate it further without hospital records."

Gary looked at him seriously, "All of this information could potentially explode into media frenzy. We need to handle this carefully."

Stair nodded his head, "I agree."

"Well, without further investigation into the claims, type me up a summary of the claims and the findings of your preliminary investigation. I will take that to the chief and discuss how we proceed."

Stair started to fidget, picking at the cracked arm on the chair, "Sounds good, boss. I will get that to you as soon as possible." Again he hesitated for a beat; then he asked, "Did you want my name or your name on it?"

Gary looked at him levelly, "My name, your initials after."

"Sure thing, it's extensive, so it may be a day or two," Stair said, as he rose and walked to the door.

"Shut my door on your way out. Thanks."

Gary Brown went back to the phone records he had been looking at. After he reviewed all those records he had proof of who had called Nelthrope the day that they took his report. The fact that Mike Martin in the Executive Protection Unit knew that he had sent officers over to interview Nelthrope, coupled with the fact that he had called Nelthrope behaving like a threat and a menace, meant there was a mole in his department. It was exactly the kind of behavior he was hired to eradicate. There was obviously someone leaking information from his department to the EPU.

After reviewing McClure's phone records, he could not prove that it was him that had informed Mike Martin that Nelthrope was making a complaint. Nor was he in any way convinced the McClure was the mole, but he knew he had one. Gary knew he had to be extremely discreet about all investigations into the EPU. But by the middle of April, he was on a mission to find out who exactly the EPU reported to.

During his weekly briefing with his boss, the Chief of Police, Jerry Oliver, he bought it up. "I've been receiving some rumors and complaints about EPU. I don't have anything official yet in writing, but they're out of control and we need to do something about it."

Jerry looked at him levelly and asked, "Who is in charge of EPU?"

"You are. I mean they work for you through your Chief of Staff, Shereece Flemming."

"Check it out."

His next stop was Shereece office. He asked her, "Are you in charge of EPU?"

She replied, "No, Assistant Chief Walter Shoulders is. "

He marched down the hall to Shoulders office, "Are you in charge of EPU?"

Shoulders looked up from his sandwich; "No, I gave it to James Bearing over at SRT."

He went back to his office and called James Bearing at SRT, "Are you in charge of EPU?"

"No way. I spent one day over at EPU and I'll never go back again."

The following day he stopped by Chief Oliver's office and said, "Nobody is in charge of EPU. That means you are. We need to get control of it."

Oliver looked at him steadily and said, "Then get control of it."

Gary wasn't thrilled that it took two days to find out who was in charge of the EPU when the Chief is the sole person who makes decisions about placing someone in charge of any department. He should have known who was in charge. The fact that he told Brown to "get control of it," could be construed as a way for him to duck his own responsibility. Not that he blamed

him for wanting to.  From what he was hearing, they were a real

handful over there in EPU.

It wasn't the first investigation he had headed that involved

members of the Executive Protection Unit. Not even the first one

that involved Officer Jones, who worked directly for the mayor.

The other investigation had to do with Jones brother being

arrested and having in his possession property that belonged to

the DPD.  In that investigation, Jones had left his badge cap at his

mother's and his brother had possession of it without his

knowledge. Jones didn't get in any trouble for that. It was well

known that Jones and the Mayor grew up together, played high

school football together and that they were close friends. At some

point Jones had been promoted to be the officer in charge of the

EPU. Although, he had acted like he was in charge of it from day

one.

Gary Brown knew this investigation was going to be a

headache.  It ticked him off that Martin had been informed of the

complaint prior to a detective taking Nelthrope's statement.  The impropriety of Martin calling Nelthrope didn't sit well with him. The fact that he had a mole in his department kept him up nights. He was going to find out who leaked the information and put an end to it.

The first draft Stair had typed came to Gary's desk on April 24th, 2003. He reviewed it thoroughly and wanted Stair to make a few changes to the verbiage of it before it was passed on to Chief Oliver.

It read:

Inter-Office Memorandum
Professional Accountability Bureau
Date: 4/30/03
To: Chief of Police Jerry A. Oliver, Sr. (Direct)
Subject: ALLEGATIONS AGAINST MAYOR KWAME M. KILPATRICK, MRS. CARLITA KILPATRICK AND MEMBERS ASSIGNED TO THE EXECUTIVE PROTECTION UNIT
From: Deputy Chief Gary A. Brown, Professional Accountability Bureau

The internal Affairs Section has received information of possible police misconduct committed by police Officers Lorenzo Jones, badge #4232, and Michael Martin, badge #425, both assigned to the Executive Protection Unit. The allegations also include Mayor Kwame M. Kilpatrick and his wife, Mrs. Carlita Kilpatrick.

On April 26th, 2003, Sergeant Shawn Wesley, badge S-369, of the Public Corruption Unit, interviewed Officer Harold Nelthrope, badge 4906, currently assigned to the seventh precinct, formerly assigned to the Executive Protection Unit. The following is a synopsis of the allegations.

Officer Nelthrope alleges that between late December 2002 and early January 2003, Officer Lorenzo Jones was seen leaving the scene of a motor vehicle accident in the area of "Half Past 3" nightclub that is located on 2458 Grand River. Officer Jones was allegedly driving a GMC Yukon SUV (which was assigned to the Mayor's security detail) when he struck a parked vehicle in the area. An unknown person recognized Officer Jones and told the possible owner of the vehicle that the person that struck his vehicle was Officer Jones and that he worked for Mayor Kwame Kilpatrick.

The owner of the vehicle allegedly called the Mayor's office regarding the incident, but it is not known if any action was taken in the matter. It is alleged that Officer Jones subsequently took the Yukon to an unnamed repair shop on Mound Rd. in Warren, Michigan and paid for the repairs. The repair shop is alleged to be the same shop where the Mayor's Cadillac is taken for repairs.

On or about, February 7th, 2003, it is alleged that Office Michael Martin was scheduled to work a 24-hour shift (6 A.M. February 6th to 6 A.M. February 7th). It is alleged Officer Martin left his post to attend a party given by Officer Jones at the Half Past 3 nightclub. Officer Martin was still on duty and was seen consuming alcohol at the party.

It is alleged that officer Martin was involved in a motor vehicle accident after leaving this party. Officer Martin was driving vehicle code #030016, a 2003 black Ford Crown Victoria, which is assigned to the Executive protection Unit. The vehicle did sustain three flat tires and some type of under carriage damage on or about this date.

It is also alleged that an officer from the Executive Protection Unit was ordered to Officer Martin's home to change a flat tire on the vehicle that morning around 9:30 A.M. The officer allegedly observed that the vehicle had three flat tires and may have had some damage on one of the quarter panels. The officer also allegedly noticed that Officer Martin was intoxicated and he left his weapon in the car. Officer Martin supposedly told the officer that he hit something in the street. The vehicle was towed to the Livernois garage.

Officer Nelthrope's source advised him that upon Officer Martin's arrival at the EPU office, he began looking for any paperwork regarding the accident. A preliminary investigation into the merits of this allegation conducted by the Public Corruption Unit revealed that a call to Department of Public Works (DPW) was placed to dispatch a tow-truck on February 7th, 2003 at 9:25 A.M. because the vehicle had two flat tires. DPW personnel at the Russell Ferry Garage stated that the vehicle, 030016, had three flat tires and undercarriage damage.

The vehicle was sent to Riverside Ford because the check engine light was on and there was a noise coming from the engine. A Ford motor Company representative took custody of the vehicle and conveyed it to an unknown location for unknown reasons. The vehicle was returned to Russell Ferry Garage. The vehicle also travelled to the Livernois Garage and Jergenson Ford for additional repairs.

A preliminary search by DPW personnel at both Livernois and Russell Ferry Garages for documents related to repairs made by DPW to the vehicle revealed that the documents could not be located. The DPW also requested a report from the EPU to explain the damage to the vehicle, but never received one.

A cursory check of accident reports filed at the records unit for February 6th-8th did not reveal a report was filed. DPW personnel stated that they received a telephone call from the director of DPW to fix the vehicle, despite the fact that there was no accident report.

It is alleged that both Officers Jones and Martin frequently visit the Half Past 3 nightclub while on duty and it is well known by the patrons that they work for Mayor Kilpatrick and that the officers occasionally cause disturbances in the nightclub.

It was also reported that Officer Jones and Martin submitted overtime reports for as much as 50 to 60 hours worked during a pay period without even working the required regular time hours prior to earning the overtime. It is alleged that both officers used the approval stamp of former Second Deputy Chief Ronald Flemming to approve the overtime without Second Deputy Chief Flemming's knowledge and approval.

Officer Nelthrope also alleged that a private party took place at the Manoogian Mansion prior to the move in of the first family. He alleges Mayor Kilpatrick was present at the party and that the party featured female nude dancers. He alleges Mrs. Kilpatrick arrived unexpectedly at the mansion and observed the mayor, his friends and the dancers. He further stated that a fight ensued between Mrs. Kilpatrick and the dancers and that the dancers received injuries that required medical attention. It is alleged that the dancer was treated at St. John's hospital and also that the Executive Protection Unit confiscated all activity logs from the seventh precinct. Officer Nelthrope stated that he found out about this incident the following day. Officer Nelthrope would not give the exact date of the alleged party.

Officer Nelthrope stated that he has maintained a diary of events that he observed while assigned to the Executive Protection Unit. He further stated that he revealed these allegations to the Detroit Office of the Federal Bureau of Investigation. Supervisory Special Agent Michael O'Conner, the Agent in charge of the Public Corruption Unit of the Detroit Office of the Federal Bureau of Investigation was contacted and confirmed that Officer Nelthrope has not contacted his office. Based on the nature of the allegations, the F.B.I. has not opened a case into Officer Nelthrope's allegations.

It should be noted that Officer Nelthrope was assigned to the Executive Protection Unit at the bequest of former Second Deputy Chief Ronald Flemming. Officer Nelthrope was involuntarily transferred out of the Executive Protection Unit, following the dismissal of Second Deputy Chief Flemming. It should also be noted that Officer Nelthrope claims to have no firsthand knowledge of these events, with the exception of receiving a phone call to have a member of the Executive

Protection Unit to respond to Officer Martin's home to change the flat tires and that Officer Martin was scheduled to work from 6:00 A.M. to 6:00 A.M. on February 6th, 2003.

The most serious allegation that Officer Nelthrope made is that Mrs. Carlita Kilpatrick was involved in a physical altercation with a female dancer, causing bodily injury requiring medical attention. If this allegation is proven to be fact, the potential for assault charges to be filed against Mrs. Carlita Kilpatrick as well as potential obstruction of justice charges and or misconduct against anyone found to have collected and destroyed activity logs will warrant national headlines and severely damage the political future of Mayor Kilpatrick.

The second most serious of the allegations is the alleged falsification of timesheets in order to gain financially from the payment of overtime.

The Internal Affairs Section has on more than one occasion investigated similar allegations. Exhaustive fraud investigations in the recent past with evidence gained through covert surveillance and extensive review of documents have been conducted and presented to the Wayne County Prosecutor. On each occasion, the warrant requests have been denied. This abuse of the system is viewed by the prosecutor as an internal failure to properly supervise and put in place the proper controls, and not a successfully prosecutable criminal offense

The third most serious allegation is the allegation that Officer Jones was involved in a hit and run accident. This allegation if investigated and found to be true could result in the misdemeanor criminal prosecution of Officer Jones.

The fourth most serious allegation is the allegation that Officer Martin was involved in a single motor vehicle accident and failed to properly report it. There is no proof that could prove or refute whether or not Officer Martin was intoxicated at the time of the accidents and depending on what the object was, whether or not driving over an object in the roadway can be deemed an accident by state statute. The allegation that Officer Martin left a handgun in the car may result in a number of departmental charges if proven beyond a preponderance of the evidence.

The fifth most serious allegation is the practice of Officers Jones and Martin drinking alcoholic beverages while on duty.

Regardless of blood alcohol content, the odor of intoxicants on the breath of a member deems that member unfit for duty, a clear violation of department policy.

Based on the serious nature of these allegations and the potential damage to the reputation and good standing within the community and the nation of the Mayor of the City of Detroit, the Honorable Kwame Kilpatrick, the Mayors wife, Mrs. Carlita Kilpatrick and two Detroit Police officers assigned to the Executive Protection Unit, I am submitting this memorandum for your review. At your direction, the Professional Accountability Bureau is poised to conduct a thorough and impartial investigation into this matter.

Gary A. Brown

Deputy Chief

Professional Accountability Bureau

GAB:brs

Gary Brown took the memo to Chief Oliver's office and tried to give it to him. The Chief took it and glanced down at the memo, and handed it right back to Brown. "I don't want this; you're going to have to rewrite this."

He didn't care for the word "poised" in the document, but a total re-write? "Re-write it?"

"Take out the allegations regarding the mayor's wife. They have not been substantiated. Put the rest of the information in a bullet style memo and then I'll look at it.

** (This particular memo, to be given directly to Chief Oliver was dated April 30th, 2003. The same day that Tamara Greene lost her life.)**

Chapter 9.

Gary Brown

"When you turn on the light, the roaches get to crawling"

(A quote by: Former Detroit Police Chief Jerry Oliver)

After his meeting with the chief, Gary made a visit to the FBI. He needed to know if Nelthrope had asked them to begin an investigation based on his allegations. He wanted someone from the outside to investigate this matter, anyway. Unfortunately, they turned him down, citing the reasons relating to jurisdiction. They also confirmed to him that Nelthrope had not contacted them. The chief had indicated to him that he wanted that information in the memo.

On May 2nd, 2003, Gary Brown received a call from Shereece Flemming, Jerry Oliver's Chief of Staff, "Hi Gary. I am calling you regarding some changes."

"Changes to what?"

"Christine Beatty is now in charge of the Executive Protection Unit and wants to be informed and present any time you interview anyone under Garrity provisions or for any other reason."

Garrity rights protect public employees from being compelled to incriminate themselves during investigative inquiries by their employers.

Gary blew up; "That is unacceptable and that is not going to happen."

She continued to speak; "It will happen, Gary. Forward any information you have on any investigation into the staff of EPU to Christine Beatty."

He was un-phased; "That's not going to happen. This phone call is inappropriate."

Shereece hung up the telephone on him. Having no intentions on following the instructions of Ms. Flemming, he started to include them in his report. It was highly inappropriate that Christine Beatty, the Mayors Chief of Staff, would involve herself in the matters that related to an investigation of improprieties of the EPU. And the fact that Christine had Shereece, Jerry Oliver's Chief of Staff, phone him about it, instead of calling him personally, let him know that Christine knew she was out of line. It also gave him pause for thought. He wondered if Chief Oliver had been advised of the changes that Christine Beatty was trying to make.

He went back to the bullet style memo he was working on for Chief Oliver. The one he was told to re-construct from the one dated 4/30/2003. Brian had given him new information to incorporate and he was doing as he had been ordered. He had to take out any mention of a party, dancers or an altercation with Mrs. Kilpatrick prior to turning it in to the Chief. From the content of the phone call he just received from Shereece Flemming, he had a gut feeling that, although the Chief didn't want a copy of the memo dated 4/30/03, that Christine Beatty had a copy of it, if that was possible. How else would she even know about any investigation he was conducting into purported misdeeds of the members of the EPU? *Anyone being interviewed had to go through her? Over my dead body!*

The original memo was five pages long; it took Brown a few days of tweaking it to get it down to two pages, with bullet points and removing the information he was advised to remove. The

new memo read:

To: Chief of Police, Jerry A. Oliver, Sr. Direct
Subject: Information   - Confidential
From: Gary A. Brown

This memorandum is to inform you that on Friday March 28th, 2003, Detroit Police Officer, Harold Nelthrope, badge #4906, currently assigned to the 7th precinct, requested to meet concerning a personal matter and he only wanted to meet in his home. The following bullet points highlight the discussion and conversation between Officer Nelthrope, Inspector McClure and Lieutenant Lawrence.

- He made it a point of telling us he was wearing a bullet proof vest because he didn't trust many police officers.
- That some of the information he shared might be third party.
- Officer Nelthrope keeps a book and notes' regarding matters that he thinks are important and issue that border on police misconduct by two members of the Executive Protection Detail. These members are Officer Lorenzo Jones, badge #4232, and Michael Martin, badge #425
- He mentioned that Officer Jones, in late December, 2002, early January, 2003, while off duty had a traffic accident while driving his department assigned Yukon after leaving Half Past 3 nightclub and then fled the scene.
- Officer Nelthrope talked about in January/February 2003, Officers Jones and Martin were paid for overtime they didn't work and while travelling out of town.
- That on or about February 6, 2003 Officer Martin, while working his 24-hour shift and after dropping the Mayor at the Mayor's quarters, left to attend a party given by Officer Jones at Half Past 3 nightclub.
- That Officer Martin was observed drinking at the party.

- That on February 7, 2003, when Officer Nelthrope arrived at the mansion, he received a telephone call from Officer Martin to have someone assist with changing a flat tire on his assigned department vehicle. Officer Martin's gun was left in the car. That Officer (Johnson) went to assist and noted that Officer Martin was drunk as a skunk and that his vehicle (a new Crown Victoria) possibly hit something and had to be towed to Livernois Garage.
- A cursory look into this matter is being done by members of the Internal Affairs Section.

It is apparent that the majority of Officer Nelthrope's information is coming from a third party. It is also apparent that he is receiving information from a current member of the Executive Protection Unit. Officer Nelthrope states that he is happy with his new assignment; however his motivation for coming forward at this time is suspect.

Finally, Officer Nelthrope has indicated that he has forwarded this information to the FBI. A Check regarding that fact reveals that at this time the FBI as not received any information from Officer Nelthrope.

The Internal Control Division's mission involves the investigation of criminal cases. Based on the volume of force issues facing this Department and the Professional Accountability Bureau, at this time the writer recommends that priority dictate that our time would be better utilized on reducing our open case load. The issues surrounding these events involve administrative and departmental issues that can be addressed through proactive supervision. Therefore, unless directed by the Chief of Police, no further action will be taken regarding these issues.

Gary A. Brown

Deputy Chief

Professional Accountability

Finally, he had it worded precisely the way he had been directed to. Chief Oliver signed it May 6th, 2003 with the handwritten notation, "No further investigation directed at this time."

On May 9th, he received a call from Chief Oliver. "Gary, I need to meet with you now."

Gary was surprised to get a call that late on a Friday from the Chief; "It's after five, can't it wait?"

Chief Jerry Oliver answered him; "No it can't. Head back to your office and I'll meet you there."

Gary knew an order when he heard one. He turned his car around and headed back to the office; "Sure thing."

Chief Oliver was waiting for him when he got back to his office. His face was red and he looked somber. He wasted no time getting to the point; "Gary, your employment here is terminated, effective immediately."

He handed him a letter of termination.

"You're firing me?" He was shocked. "Why?"

"Mayor Kilpatrick and Christine Beatty just left my office and insisted I terminate you effective immediately. I don't know why, but I will find out."

He thought; *what the hell is it to Christine Beatty?* But he said, "Oh, I assure you, I will find out as well."

"You know I have the utmost respect for you, Gary." He looked at the floor. "They said there were things going on in your department that I am not aware of, is there anything you need to talk to me about?"

He thought about the conversation that he had a few days prior with Shereece Flemming; "It wouldn't change a thing. Where is my computer?"

"All of the computers from this department have been confiscated. I think this a huge mistake Gary, I feel terrible doing this."

Gary looked incredulous; "My computer has been confiscated? Who made the decision to take my computer?"

Jerry gave him the answer that he had been given; "It's standard procedure, Gary."

"That's bull-shit and you know it. Let me guess, Christine Beatty?"

The Chief's face reddened even more, he replied, "It doesn't change anything, Gary."

Gary shook his head in disbelief, "No, I don't suppose it does. Some people are going to do whatever they want and screw anyone that gets in the way, right Chief?

Gary Brown shook his hand as he stood up to leave his office for the last time, "I know it isn't you, Chief, we worked hard here and we can be proud of what we accomplished. It's beyond sad that it had to end this way."

"Yes, it is." The two men walked out of the office together. Gary Brown got to his car, but before he got in, he turned and took one long last look at the building where he gave so much of his life. He shook his head with resignation and decided the first call that he was going to make would be to a lawyer.

Chapter 10.

Marian Stevenson

April 30th, 2003, 3:30 A.M., Homicide Detective Marian Stevenson picked up the work phone ringing on her night-stand, "This is Stevenson."

"We have a homicide victim, possible gunshot wounds, Santa Rosa and Oakman."

Tossing the blankets off, she turned on her lamp and sat up, "Ok, I'm on my way."

It was not unusual for her to get up at any hour of the day or night when she was working re-call rotation. She had to take the call no matter what time it came in if she was the next one up for a case. She had been working almost three years in homicide and more than eighteen years as a police officer, she was used to odd hours. Her conviction rate of ninety-seven percent spoke for itself. The best of the best in homicide, she loved her job.

It took her less than ten minutes to put her uniform on, put her hair back in a ponytail, brush her teeth and get out of the door.

She arrived on the scene less than a half an hour later and started taking notes as the evidence techs took pictures and collected the physical evidence. She wrote in her spiral note book: car running, passenger door open, bullet holes in side of car.

Writing in her spiral-bound tablet all the things she noticed when she arrived on the scene was her ingrained habit. She relied heavily on her notes. She knew she would need them later to fill in her Preliminary Criminal Report, better known as a PCR.

There were two witnesses on the scene who were interviewed. One man happened to be walking by on the street when he had heard the shots. He stated that after he had heard the shots, he then saw a white SUV speeding off. The other witness on the scene was a tenant in the downstairs apartment of the house that was the closest to the scene. Apparently the passenger, Eric Mitchell, had been shot and sought help for his injuries by running to the nearest house and trying to get in it. The home owner refused to open the door to him. However, the homeowner was the one who made the 911 call reporting the incident. Lieutenant Jackson took the report from the homeowner, while

Sergeant Davis from the Special Response Squad interviewed the man that was on the street.

It was daylight by the time that they had finished their work at the crime scene and had released the body of Tamara Greene to the medical examiner. Marian went directly in to work and got started on the PCR. It wasn't long before Lt. Jackson came into work. During the morning meeting he assigned her the case as the Officer in Charge, which is commonly referred to as the OIC. She sat at her desk and started to work on the case. She started by first taking her notes from her spiral notebook and filling in the blanks on the forms that were in the case notes system on the computer.

Detective Thomas walked by her desk and commented, "I wouldn't want to be in your shoes."

She quipped back, "You couldn't fit in my shoes. "

She paid him no attention and methodically worked on the case like she would any other. It wasn't that she didn't hear the rumors, but she had grown up on the streets of Detroit and didn't put much credit in rumors. There was no reason for her to believe that the murder had anything to do with the incidents last fall.

It was hard for her to ignore them talking. She remembered it too; when the water cooler talk was that the squad had been called out to the Manoogian Mansion for a disturbance. That rumor travelled faster through the entire police department than the bird flu. The whole Detroit Police Department was aware that there was a party and supposedly an altercation involving some dancers and the mayor's wife. The gossip had flowed like an airborne pathogen. The rumor was that a police officer had also been there dancing and that the dancer that had been hurt had used the officers medical card when she received emergency medical services. The dispatch tapes were confiscated the following day by members of the EPU.

For some reason many of the officers she worked with seemingly connected Tamara Greene with that rumored party. She would have to be deaf not to hear the "shop talk". But she had no intention on working from innuendo, nor did she see a correlation between the possibility that Tamara may have been present at that party and the fact that she was gunned down on the street several months later. Stevenson had a job to do, and real leads to track and follow.

About mid-day, Marian walked down the hall to use the bathroom. As she did, a woman cop that she didn't know made a ducking motion and said, "I don't want to get close to you, I might get shot like Tammy."

Marian looked at her and replied, "You're hilarious."

She thought, *yeah right, cops are so funny.* She was used to off color humor in the department. Homicide detectives often had an odd sense of humor. They referred to the rods that they placed in bullet holes to get the trajectory angle 'forks' as in, "put a fork in him, he's done." It was hard not get somewhat immune to the environment. A healthy distance had to be maintained in order not to let the job affect a person's psyche. It was tough to see some of the things they saw on a regular basis. Off kilter humor helped them cope with the job. She went back to her desk and continued making a list of the people she wanted to interview: Tamara's family members, her co-workers, Eric Mitchell..

Later that afternoon, she was told that Lt. Jackson had been promoted to squad leader. Lt. Bowman was given his position. Lt. Bowman was now her immediate supervisor.

After lunch, she stopped by Jackson's new office as he was unpacking his things, "Moving on up. Congratulations."

He looked up from what he was doing and smiled, "Thanks, Stevenson."

She liked Billy Jackson and was happy that he had gotten the promotion, "You deserved it."

He smiled at her and she headed back down the hall to her desk. They all fell into an easy routine over the next few weeks. Bowman was helpful and easy to work both with and for, so it was a good arrangement.

He occasionally assisted her in tracking down leads that came in on her case. He even accompanied her when she interviewed witnesses at times. Normally all of the members of her department worked together as a team, but volunteers to even take a message for her about this case were hard to find. There were people in her department that outright refused to work on the case.

There was only one other female detective that worked on the squad. During one of the morning briefings she said, "I don't want anything to do with that case. I like my job. I don't want to be transferred and I definitely don't want to be fired. I have kids, I don't need the headache."

While Marian would have liked to have seen the squad leader follow up on why Sandy felt that way about the case and put an end to the gossip and negative environment surrounding it, the only reply to her statement during the meeting was. "We all need to remember we are investigating a murder, not a party. Let's keep focused on what we're doing."

Marian knew Sandy lived in Belleville and was the sole provider for her kids. She didn't blame her for feeling that way. Not after all of the comments and warnings she had gotten since taking the case. Especially after all the media attention the case was getting. The news every night was reporting about the murder victim, the mayor's staff and Gary Brown's wrongful termination lawsuit. Two other investigators from internal affairs had also been transferred. Demoted was a better word to describe it than transferred. When an officer gets sent to precinct to work patrol, it's a demotion. Sandy's concerns were valid.

The job was important to Marian. To stop working on a case because of pressure was never going to be an option she would consider. She loved what she did for a living. When she started working in homicide she felt like she had stepped into her destiny. Her faith was an important part of her life and she had faith that what she was doing was both important and right. She never doubted that God would protect her as she did her job.

As she worked the case, she kept Lt. Bowman informed of her progress and direction, potential leads and persons of interest. A few potential suspects were ruled out, one by one. When she arrived back to the office after collecting some statements one afternoon she found a video tape on her desk. It was footage of Tamara's funeral; Reverend Ken Hampton had dropped it off with the message that it may be helpful with the investigation.

She picked up her phone, dialed Bowman's extension and asked him, "Did you see the Reverend when he dropped off the video of Tamara Greene's funeral?"

"No, I think Jackson talked to him. You have the video? Meet me in the conference room and we'll have a look at it."

Bowman was waiting for her in the conference room and they watched the funeral video together.

As she took notes she asked him, "You see what I see, right?"

Bowman replied, "Yes, I do."

She asked him, "Do you know any of them by name?"

"I'm not sure of names, but I have seen them around here."

There were at least five members of the Detroit police department that she had recognized at Tamara's funeral. She recognized the faces but not all of their names. She would track those down later and possibly question them about how they knew Tamara and why they were present at her funeral. The three she recognized were Officers Jones and Martin from EPU and Officer Davis from the Special Response Unit. There were several other people that she recognized, it was a large funeral. She was surprised how many people she knew personally that were in attendance. Her hairdresser was even there. *Interesting, Davis was a responder at the crime scene; he didn't mention that he knew the victim that morning.*

She looked at Bowman with raised brows, "Tamara must have known a lot of cops."

He replied dryly, "Apparently so, let me know if you need help tracking them down."

"I will let you know when I get to that, I would like to interview Eric Mitchell again and still have a long list of friends and co-workers to talk to first."

Eric was a hard one to pin down for an interview. He would not meet in her office on Beubien. He insisted she meet him at a Body shop on Telegraph Road. Bowman went with her to interview him. He was nervous and his eyes darted around as she took his information. What little information he had did not prove to be all that helpful. She had a feeling he knew more than he was telling her. He probably saw who the shooter was, but he didn't give them much of a description. Marian knew that pressing him wasn't going to help, so she decided to interview him again at a later time. He was obviously scared and not ready to talk.

It was not in her nature to give up on any case, no matter how hard the leads were to chase down. This one was no different. The constant media attention was nothing but a distraction. She had to work off the facts and the evidence. She took two trips to Ohio to meet with Tamara's mother and had turned in the paperwork to take a trip to Alabama to speak with her grandmother. They had spoken on the phone and she thought it might be worth the trip as the grandmother said she had some information that she didn't want to talk about over the phone.

The Michigan State Police was conducting an investigation into the rumored party at the Manoogian Mansion and alleged misconduct within the EPU, as was the Attorney General's office. She knew Lt. Bowman was in communication with them about a possible connection between Tamara Greene's murder and the supposed party.

Marian would watch the nightly news and feel like she was still at work. Reporters were all over her case and a possible connection to a party. Gary Brown had filed a lawsuit claiming wrongful dismissal for investigating Nelthropes' allegations of improprieties within the EPU. The mayor called Nelthrope a liar and said his whistleblower lawsuit had no merit. The mayor and his Chief of Staff, Christine Beatty, also publically discredited Brown, but Chief Oliver stated that it was his decision to fire him. It was a confusing press conference. The press was on a feeding frenzy. She thought: *how odd that Chief Oliver admitted it was his decision to fire Gary Brown and yet had no answer when the reporters asked him why he had been fired.*

The news that Brian Stair was given Brown's position as head of Professional Accountability Bureau, and that McClure had been transferred back into the department travelled fast. Stair was the one that typed up the memo for Gary Brown that Chief Oliver said he never got until after Brown had been fired. Tamara was in all the papers and the nightly news for months. As was the mayor and his staff. After awhile she quit watching the news, it was the only way to leave work at work.

She was still occasionally razzed by her follow officers, just general comments like, "I wouldn't want to be you." Or, "I'm not sitting next to you." Those types of comments were getting old. It may have been funny at first, but it was wearing off fast.

After several months had gone by, the Michigan State police and Attorney general closed their investigation into the alleged EPU misconduct and publically announced the supposed party was an "urban legend". It seemed premature to her, but her concern was her own case. She wasn't investigating a party or the mayoral protection unit, she was investigating a murder. She was making good progress on the case and had ruled out several potential suspects. *I suppose it's time to start interviewing the members of the police department that attended her funeral and see if any leads surface from that avenue.*

She went into work one Monday in October of 2003 and the first thing she noticed was that the lock box containing her computer floppy disks had been pried open.

She said out loud to anyone in earshot, "Who couldn't wait for me to get to work to lend them a floppy disk?"

No one replied to her. Upon further inspection she noticed the four floppy disks that were labeled Tamara Greene were missing from the box.

Her eyes flashed around the room to her co-workers desk-tops; "Who stole my floppy disks?"

Again no one replied to her. She booted up her computer and realized her hard drive had been erased. All of her case notes were missing.

She stormed into Bowman's office, "Would you have any idea who erased my computer and stole all of my floppy disks? It had a lock on it!"

Bowman looked at her and said, "I understand there was a glitch in the computer system over the weekend."

Marian looked at him with disbelief; "How many other computers in this department were affected?"

He answered her dryly, "Apparently it was only yours."

"Well, all of my notes are gone. My floppies contained copies of my notes also, and they are missing. The lock was pried off from the box I kept my floppy disks in."

Bowman advised her, "Do the best you can to reconstruct the case from your activity logs and your notebook, that's all I can suggest. Is there anything else I can help you with?"

"No sir." She walked back to her desk and worked the next several days on reconstructing her notes. Several more trips had to be made interviewing co-workers that she had already interviewed. Statements that she had physically placed in the file itself were missing.

Marian began to make copies of everything and created. She began to keep a duplicate file that she kept at home in her safe. Marian also relied more on hand written notes and became selective about what she entered into the mainframe computer system that served all of the Detroit Police Department. It was shame that police officers could not be trusted. It wasn't someone who walked in from the street who compromised her investigation. It was one or more of her peers. To her, that meant that she needed to be watchful and careful about whom she talked to and trusted. Her job was operation fish-bowl and she knew it. But as long as she had the support of Bowman and Lt. Jackson, it didn't bother her. She was from Detroit, and cops that weren't on the up and up didn't surprise her one bit.

Later on that week, she reached into her cabinet for the physical file. She was going to review the note that the Reverend had left when he dropped the video off of the funeral; that and Jackson's handwritten note from his conversation with the Reverend. The entire file was gone from her metal file cabinet, which had been locked. *You have to be kidding me! This is getting ridiculous.*

She walked into Bowman's office, "Do you have any idea where the case file is for Tamara Greene?"

He looked at her and shook his head from side to side and rolled his eyes, "Lt. Jackson is keeping it in his office now. I had to use my key to retrieve it for him. He picked it up this morning, if you need something from it let me know and I'll get it from him."

Air rushed from her mouth in exasperation, "Are you kidding me?"

Shaking his head again, he answered her, "No, I am not kidding you. Next week they might have me blind-fold you when you clock in, and see how you can do solving the murder like pin the tail on the donkey." He chuckled awkwardly at his own joke. It wasn't funny.

He went on to say, "It is what it is, you might as well just get back to work."

She didn't respond to his try at humor, "Why are they doing this? You don't screw around with the file of a murder investigation. Removing documents and erasing my computer files is a serious offense. I see it as obstructing justice as it relates to the investigation of a murder. This is serious, Bowman, and I don't like it one bit."

He looked at her with a half-smile and one raised eyebrow and replied, "You are asking me why someone is doing this? Why do you think? The best thing for us to do right now is continue consistently performing our job duties to the best of our ability."

He certainly had a valid point. She didn't know what to say in response to that. Bowman said a lot when he said those words, loaded with advice that would serve them both well. Protocols had already been circumvented with this homicide investigation.

She was smart enough to keep her opinions to herself and weigh her words carefully, as Bowman himself had done, "I'm going to need to see the photos from the crime scene; did they make it into the file yet?"

Bowman seemed relieved that she changed gears; "I'll check it out, I know there's a back-log and it has been taking longer than usual to get pictures."

Marian went on to say; "I'm also going to need to see the statements from the bartender and the co-workers. The bartender gave up some interesting information."

Bowman smiled at her, "Ok, make a list of what you need and I'll get it all at the same time."

Standing up, as if to walk out, she quipped, "Why don't you just get me the file?"

He shook his head and looked at her, "You know I can't do that. I don't like this anymore than you do."

Heading back to her desk, she took two steps, turned and said "Ok, I'll have a list of the things I need in ten minutes. I do appreciate your help, you know?"

"I know, keep your head up, things have a way of working out."

After she took a seat at her desk that had seen better days, she looked at her dingy coffee cup and drifted off into her thoughts for several long minutes. Marian felt blocked. She had to fight off a wave of depression about the recent changes in her work environment. Her resolve started to come back to her as she sat there. If she had to butt her head up against a brick wall every day to solve this case, then that is what she would do. Now she had to start the investigation from scratch for the third time. It was going to be a long day and a longer investigation, if that was how she had to work. Marian reminded herself that she was no quitter, and encouraged herself with the Bible verse that had popped into her mind, Philippians 1:6, "He that has begun a good work in you will continue to perform it until the day of Christ Jesus." It was her life verse and was a timely reminder to her that she wasn't in this alone. She let out a long sigh and decided to get a fresh cup of coffee before she started on her list.

The coffee did the trick, she perked right up. After she got the list together of what she needed, she took it to Bowman, "Here's the list boss."

Bowman took the list from her, looked at his watch, and told her, "Lt. Jackson is in a meeting, he'll be back this afternoon. I can't access the file until he gets back. I have to leave at two for an appointment. I'm hoping I can get your stuff to you before I leave."

It was understandable, with the file in Jackson's office, access to it revolved around his and Bowman's schedule. There wasn't much that could be done about that.

She replied, "I'll look through my notes and see if there are any leads I can follow up on while I wait."

*Someone with a lot of pull has an interest in blocking my investigation. The fact that my computer was wiped clean the same day the floppy disks came up missing. The bull-crap excuse*

*about how the case-notes that were posted in the main server*

*disappeared the same day. Looks like all of the rumors have*

*some substance. I'm going to solve this murder case if it leads me*

*to the doorstep of the Manoogian Mansion. Dear Lord, help me.*

*You know what I'm up against, keep me safe.*

For the next week or so she worked through Bowman, who

had to go to Jackson to access the file. Her time was spent trying

to reconstruct her missing notes from the computer "glitch" and

the missing floppy disks. Most of her notes were handwritten at

that point. Her file at home had just been started three days prior,

so that wasn't much help. Marian didn't trust that the paper trail

of her investigation would not be compromised again. She

continued to make two copies of her notes, one copy for the file

in Jackson's office and one copy for her home file. She hid the

file at home in a safe that was behind a false wall in her

basement. It was safe; under lock and key. Discretion was used in

every action she took; she entered select generic information into

the case-notes on the main-frame computers. There was enough gossip in the department about her and the case. To give them more fodder was not something she was interested in doing. Trust of her co-workers was a thing of the past.

She sat down at her desk and went back to work. A coworker walked by and said under his breath, "I'd be careful."

She looked up and said, "Excuse me?"

"I didn't say anything." Hearing that reply she thought, *whatever.*

Filling in the blanks from her activity logs and her spiral notebook was tedious and consumed at lot of her time, but she plugged away at it with tenacity. She was determined to solve this case. As the weeks went on it became more difficult for her to access the case file. Apparently it had been moved to the third floor where Chief Oliver and his staff worked. The murder file had been removed from the homicide department completely, which was unheard of. Never had she seen any case handled in the manner that this one was handled. Her resolution was to do her job the best that she could, and roll with the punches as they came. Her personal decision to hold fast to her integrity and not quit, no matter what the circumstances, allowed her the strength to continue to do her job and work around the roadblocks.

Once the case file had been moved, yet again, the process for her to access it had also been changed, again. The chain had gotten longer, now she had to request what she needed from Bowman, who would then request it from Lt. Jackson, who would then contact the third floor where an unknown individual would retract what she needed from the file. Then the document would pass through the same four or more hands in reverse to make it to her desk for review. They refused to send her the whole file, just the specific item she asked for; and much like the game telephone, by the time it went through four people it wasn't accurate. So there were times she received information that differed from what she had asked for. Then the whole process had to start all over again to get the document that she had requested the first time. It was quite a process and to her knowledge as an eighteen year veteran of the police department, it had never happened before. Her tenacity and patience paid off, after a few weeks of working in this manner, she had, for the most part, reconstructed the file.

Arriving to work a few weeks later, she noticed everyone in the office whispering. When she walked back toward her desk a hush fell over the room. She didn't know what it was about and didn't ask. Marian Stevenson wasn't one to stand around and gossip, she had a lot of work to do and a case to solve. She had been assigned new cases in addition to the Tamara Greene case, which still had leads to follow. Next on her "to do" list was to identify all of the police officers that were in attendance of the funeral and start the interview process with them. She had waited until she had exhausted all other leads before she turned her focus to those inside the department.

Lt. Jackson stopped by her desk, "We are moving the Greene case to cold case files. I'm going to need your spiral notebook, logbook and anything else pertinent to the case."

Her face showed her surprise as she looked at him, "I am still working on that case. Why would it be moved to cold case files?"

"It just is, I'm sure you have other work to do," was his curt reply.

He stood there tapping his foot while she gathered the things he requested.

"My spiral notebook is my own personal property. It does not belong to the Detroit Police Department."

He shook his head back and forth, "No, we're going to need it. I need everything that contains any and all information related to the case and your investigation."

She turned it over to him reluctantly. *This is messed up. Someone doesn't want this case solved. Protocols have been thrown out the window from day one. Let cold case deal with it. Let their computers be hacked and deal with the headache of the difficulty of working on this case! UGH. Forget it.*

Marian asked him, "Who will it be assigned to?"

"I am not sure which detective it is. I was instructed to gather everything up and keep it in my office and that's what I'm doing."

She understood that Jackson was just following orders, "Ok, if the cold case investigator has any questions, and I'm sure he will, I will be more than available to help him in any way that I can."

His expression seemed genuine to her when he said to her, "We appreciate all of your hard work on this. "

She looked at Jackson levelly, "Of course."

She thought of all that had transpired since April 30th, the day that she was called in the middle of the night to respond to the shooting. And the events that had transpired since the very moment that she took the case. As Jackson walked away with a box that contained over a year's worth of her work she thought, *Good riddance. It is unheard of to move a murder that was still under investigation to cold case. Generally it is at the two year mark if there are no more leads to follow. That is not the case and it is obvious someone wants this left alone. The best thing for me to do is to let it go.*

She picked up her phone and dialed Bowman's extension, "Hey boss, let's go out to lunch today. It's on me."

There was no hesitation on his end, he replied, "Sounds good, I want to talk to you about something."

She already had a plan in mind, "Let's drive separately and meet at Lafayette Coney Island on Michigan Ave around 1pm. Work for you?"

He quickly agreed, "That'll work."

They pulled into the parking lot at the same time, 1 P.M. sharp. It was packed, but that was not unusual. Ford motor company executives piled into the restaurant 'en masse. Dressed in their khaki pants and button down shirts, they tried not to get chili on their clothes. They rushed through their lunches, thumbing through copies of Metro Times with one hand while stuffing onion rings in their mouth with the other. One thing for certain, the service was fast there and they catered well to the crowd of regulars. The owners were well aware that their clientele had limited time to eat on their lunch breaks.

After they had sat down at a table that was still slightly wet, a harried looking waitress brought two ice waters and took their coffee order.

167

Marian looked at Bowman, "I can't believe they moved my case already."

He looked at her and raised his eyebrows, "Well, they gave it to Godbold and he doesn't even want the damn thing."

The waitress was back in a flash with their coffee. She had her pen and an order pad in her hand, "Are you two ready to order?"

Marian smiled and thought, *she doesn't want us taking up her table all afternoon, bless her heart. She needs to keep these tables moving so she can make some money.*

"Two chili dogs with everything for each of us and an order of onion rings to split."

Bowman didn't have to look at the menu to order; they ate at there as often as the Ford workers did and he knew what she always ordered.

She blew on her coffee; it was way too hot for her to drink yet, ""What's Godbold's beef?"

"He told me that his nephew was screwing her and that he knew her. Not well, but he did know her. I don't know if that's true or not, but he definitely didn't want to take the case. He's pissed that he got it."

Her eyebrows raised and she gave him a surprised look, "Did they give him the file?"

He shook his head and told her, "No, they are still keeping it under lock and key."

Finally sipping on her coffee, she asked him, "So, who decided to move the case to cold files?"

The waitress returned with their food. They thanked her and immediately dug in to their Coney dogs. They waited for her to walk away before they spoke again.

Bowman was still on his first bite when he replied to her question, "I think it was brass, Jackson didn't look pleased when I asked him about it."

"You know, he is just following orders. Things are out of his hands too, you know. We'll see where it goes now. I think someone with a lot of influence doesn't want this murder solved."

He nodded his head in agreement, "Yeah, I don't think Jackson wants anything to do with what is going on. It's best if we just let it go now."

Marian readily agreed, "Jacksons caught between and rock and a hard place. I'm glad I'm not in his shoes. I heard that's why Chief Oliver retired when he did, the same kind of thing."

"Yeah, I heard the same thing. He didn't sign on to work for Christine Beatty. The Gary Brown incident was bullshit. His hands were tied."

She leaned in closer to him over the table and spoke to him in a quiet tone, "You know who I was going to start questioning next. I waited until I had no other leads. I wonder if Godbold will pick up where I left off on working the case. I'll help him in any way that I can."

Bowman had a doubtful look on his face, "I doubt he will get very far. Look what happened to all of your notes on the case."

Marian leaned back in the booth and replied, "Oh well, whatever happens with it, I can say that I did my best to solve the case. My badge is clean."

He lifted one brow as he said, "My gut tells me that not everyone that works for the Detroit Police Department can say the same thing. I think it was a cop that killed her."

With that statement from Bowman she wiped the corners of her mouth with her napkin and tossed it onto her empty plate. Chills went over her body from head to toe as his words rang over and over in her head. She had no intentions on voicing her opinion about what he had just said.

Holding out her arms for him to see she said, "That just gave me goose bumps."

They finished their lunch without another word. Marian broke the silence, "Well, are you ready to get back to work?"

He picked up the check, facing down on the table, and glanced at the total as he pulled his wallet out of his back pocket with his other hand.

He tossed some one dollar bills on the table for a tip and told her, "Don't worry, I've got this one."

Marian reached for the check and said, "I invited you."

"Nah, I got it."

"Thanks boss, see you back at the office."

It was three days before Godbold called her and they set up a meeting to discuss the case in his office. She told him the direction that the investigation had been headed; spent quite a bit of time with him going over the methodical way that she had of eliminating suspects. She had given him all of the information that she had garnered during her investigation. And she made sure that he knew she had still been waiting for approval to go and interview the grandmother in Alabama. That was the only piece of information that she had for him that he had bothered to write down. He seemed uninterested in her suggestion to interview the staff of the EPU. *Well, I never got close enough to figure out the connection between his administration and the case, if there even is one.*

It was his baby; he could investigate it how he saw fit. It was out of her hands. He wasn't going to get very far investigating without the physical file in his possession anyway. She had other cases to work on.

The following day when she reported to work Bowman wasn't present in the morning meeting.

She noticed his office was empty. She walked to Lt. Jackson's office. When she knocked on his door he told her, "Come in, have a seat."

She sat in the stained chair across the desk from where he sat, "Thanks, do you know where Bowman is?"

He looked at her and said, "Bowman has been transferred to a precinct."

She moved to the edge of the chair and asked him, "Do you know *why* he was transferred?"

He reached into his desk for a pen, "He had a big mouth."

She looked back at him with a puzzled expression, "He was transferred because he had a big mouth, sir?"

His face turned red and he pointed the pen in his hand in her direction and said, "It is none of your business why he was transferred. I follow orders, just like everyone else around here. Don't you have a murder cases to solve?"

She stood up, knowing it was time to leave his office, "Yes, sir."

The way it appeared to her is that he was embarrassed and didn't want to talk about it. It was obvious to her that this was not his decision. It was also obvious that he was not happy about it. If she asked him anymore about it she knew that he wouldn't answer her. He wouldn't answer to a subordinate.

"Is there anything else I can help you with?" He motioned toward his door.

Walking toward the door she replied respectfully, "No, sir."

*They gave Bowman a demotion for talking to reporters? Lt. Bowman was awesome. I can't believe they are demoting him. He is the only one helping me with this case. Un-frickin-beieivable. I'm next. With Chief Oliver resigning and Bully-Cummings now chief, Bowman transferred, Brown fired, I'm better off not to have anything else to do with it. It's time for me to keep my nose to the grindstone, focus on my cases and forget about Tamara Greene.*

What Bowman had said the day they went out to lunch together kept running through her mind. His theory, if it were true, would make a lot of things make sense. From the way the other officers treated her, to the computer being hacked and her investigative notes and floppy disks disappearing. No matter what her thoughts were on his theory, she planned on keeping them to herself until there was enough evidence to back up the claim.

It was only days later that she heard a different story about why Bowman was transferred. Apparently there was a typo on a report that he had turned in to the Chief. The funny thing about that particular story was the fact that the document in question had been typed by her. Her initials were directly after his; that was the correct way to show when someone else had typed a document. There were other stories, too, about why he had been demoted. They were all different.

She wasn't surprised at all when Bowman filed a lawsuit. She had been subpoenaed to give a deposition in his case. It was not on the list of things she would like to be doing, but she would comply when the time came for her to be deposed and answer whatever questions they had for her truthfully and openly. There was no reason for Bowman's demotion. They ended up sticking to the story that there was a typo on a report he turned in. Besides the fact that she had typed the report, it was not a good reason for a transfer or demotion. If people got demoted for typos as a general rule the entire Detroit Police Department would be next in line for demotions. *They hired us to solve murders, not win spelling bees.*

She started to have panic attacks and stress related health problems not long after Bowman's demotion. Her heart would pound wildly for minutes at a time. Tension headaches became a daily malady. She had a hard time sleeping at night. Marian had to stop drinking coffee because it exacerbated her jittery feeling.

The atmosphere in the office had gradually changed since the day she took the Greene case. Her co-workers had distanced themselves from her and the camaraderie that she once enjoyed had become a thing of the past. Alvin Bowman had been her ally and support system. His demotion weighed heavily on her. There was just so much on her mind.

She went to see her doctor on her Saturday off.

Marian tried to explain what she was experiencing, "My heart feels like it will beat out of my chest. It starts racing and I feel like I might have a heart attack."

The Doctor looked at her and asked her, "Have you been under a lot of pressure lately?"

"I've been working on a very high profile case for awhile now.and..uhm…yes, I have been under a lot of stress lately, at work."

Her doctor looked at her levelly and told her, "Your blood pressure is too high; I want to order a stress test and some blood work. I am going to give you some medication for anxiety. It should help with the heart palpitations. You need to consider taking a break from work. Your job is killing you.""

"Yeah, I know, thanks doc." She took the prescriptions from his hand. *This should help the symptoms, but it won't do much for the cause.*

Later that day, she was surprised to get a call on her home number from the Detroit Police Department, she wasn't on recall duty and it was Saturday.

"Hey Marian, you are being transferred out of homicide to the 9th precinct. You are to report there on Monday at 8:00 A.M."

She didn't believe the call was legitimate, "Yeah, right."

The voice went on, "I'm serious, I was told to call you and advise you to report there on Monday for duty at 8 A.M."

"For real?"

"For real."

"Does Lt. Jackson know about this?"

Without hesitation; the voice on the other end replied, "Lt. Jackson is no longer working in the homicide department either."

"Ok…..ah……uhm….thanks for the call."

*For the first time in my 20 years as a police officer I am*

*scared. I solve ninety seven percent of my cases, why would I be*

*transferred? Sending me to the roughest precinct in Detroit? It*

*doesn't make any sense. They moved Billy Jackson too, this is not*

*good.* Receiving that news sent her into another panic attack

immediately. For several minutes her heart was beating out of

control. Once it was back to normal she went to the pharmacy.

After she had gotten her prescription filled she went back

home and took one of the pills the doctor had given her. She let

her Doberman Pincer, Max, out the front door into the gated yard,

went back into the living room and turned on her TV. She

avoided the local news stations; *I've had enough of that crap.* She

settled on an old western and tried to relax and not think about

work for a few hours. Marian fell asleep on the sofa and woke up

a few hours later when she heard Max barking like crazy because

he wanted in. She let him back in the house, made some fresh

coffee and thought about the roller coaster ride that the last two

years had been.

Chapter 11.

Marian Stevenson

The weekend passed all too quickly and Monday arrived with the alarm in her ear, "Bleep. Bleep. Bleep." That signaled to her that it was time to get ready for her new assignment. She had a few extra minutes and decided to polish her shoes so she would make an impeccable first impression when she arrived at her new post. Her uniform was without spot or wrinkle and her shoes were without a scuff when she walked out of the door, a full half hour before she was scheduled to arrive at work. She swung by Tim Horton's on her way and grabbed a fresh coffee and an "everything" bagel before heading in to her new post.

Marian reported to the 9th precinct precisely at 8 A.M. as she had been instructed to do. No one looked up from their work or acted like they noticed her at all when she walked in the door. She reported to the squad leader and he wasted no time. He assigned her to a squad car immediately. He put her on patrol duty and sent her out on her own. A lot of patrol officers worked alone, she had paid her dues years ago and knew what was expected of her when she worked in that position. She was also familiar with the area of the 9th precinct as she had lived in that neighborhood for years.

The very minute she started working in the 9th precinct, events started to happen that unsettled her and were out of her scope of experience as a police officer. She made it a point to drive by her own house at least once per shift and on several occasions when she drove by she had noticed that her front gate was open. Because of Max, she never left that gate open. She would stop and shut the gate to her front yard, only to find it open again when she came back around a few hours later.

She started to receive phone calls that were hang ups several times a night. The individual would stay on the phone for long seconds just breathing into it, then they would just hang up on her. Trying to use the *69 feature on her phone was not effective in tracking who made the call; the number could not be traced. 3 A.M. seemed to be a favorite time for the offender to call. It happened too often to be a random prankster. If the same person was responsible for the gate incidents, it could be construed as stalking. She began to keep a spiral notebook, tracking the date, time and nature of each incident as it happened.

She had a strong belief in God and found herself in prayer quite often about everything that had been happening. Having a hard time getting back to sleep after her 3 A.M. calls, she lay in her bed many nights and prayed. *God, you know what I'm going through. Please keep me safe from all harm. Guide me through these dark days. I know you have this situation in the palm of your hand.*

One day, a few weeks into her new job, while she was on patrol a dispatch call came over the radio. The call was to her personal home address stating there was an armed intruder at the residence. Since she was on patrol, her job was to go there and answer the call or help provide back-up for any other officers that were on the scene. *There is no eff-ing way I am responding to this call. This is a set up. I will die if I respond to this call. Someone wants me gone. Dear God, help me! If these people are here, who is running hell?* Her heart raced.

She called back to the dispatcher, "That is my personal home address, can you please re-check the address of the complaint?

Within seconds the dispatcher's voice reverberated through the radio, she apologized, "Uhm…there must have been a mistake, the call is for an address on Southlawn."

*I was on the news last night about my investigation of the Tamara Greene case. They're trying to set me up. It's the Tamara Greene investigation. This whole city has gone crazy. I have to take medicine to deal the anxiety of living in fear of my life! For doing my job, how is this right? Dear God, Help me. Please keep me safe. God, you know what I have been through since I started working this case. I need you now like never before.*

Two short days after that incident she came home from work to find that her home had been broken into. She had been leaving her dog in the yard for most of the day to discourage the gate pranksters. Someone used that as an opportunity to break into the back door of her home. It had been completely ransacked, totally trashed. But interestingly enough the TV's and stereos were still there. She couldn't find anything missing except for a briefcase that was kept in her hall closet, her medication and one of her guns.

Another one of her pistols lay in the middle of her bed. It was a statement break-in. The clothes were all thrown out of the closets onto the floor. Both the break-in and the call to respond to her own address came just days after they had mentioned her full name on the news in connection to the scandals surrounding the mayor and Tamara Greene's murder investigation. *The mayor had a lot of friends that were very loyal. They can break in my house every day of the week, but they will never in their lives find the copies I made of my investigation. I moved that from my residence the day they moved me to the 9th precinct. I've been a cop long enough that I don't make rookie mistakes.*

An officer that she worked with in the 9th precinct took the report of her break-in and commented to her about the gun on the bed, "Marian, I don't think this was a random break-in. It's obvious someone wanted to send you a message; the gun on the bed, the fact that the TV's are still here." She knew he was right.

This cycle would continue for years, with the harassment seemingly in sync with ebb and flow of the media. Her home had been broken into three times during the time she worked in the 9th precinct. Yes, break-ins were common on the east side of Detroit, but in the 23 years she had lived in her home, her dog had always been enough of a deterrent to home invaders. Her front gate was opened on a regular basis and the prank calls continued on and off. There were several other dispatch calls to her home address while she was on patrol. She was never stupid enough to respond to any of them. Marian Stevenson continued to pray often during her stint in the 9th precinct. She had good reason to.

She knew she was a target and she knew why. It didn't make sense and it didn't have to. It was Detroit. After twenty-three years in her home and twenty-plus on the police force, she decided it was time for her to pack it in. She didn't like leaving because of the harassment, but sticking it out wasn't helping anything either. It wasn't about them winning. It wasn't about them at all. It was just time to move on and have some peace in her life. Her anxiety level, and life in general, improved greatly once she had retired and moved out of the city.

In the spring of 2010 she was subpoenaed to depose in yet another case. A case based on the premise that Tamara Greene's murder investigation was possibly thwarted or impeded. *Fat chance they will win that one in Wayne County. It's a valid case; look at all I've been through. It pretty much ruined my life, and for what? Because some people think their own reputation is more important than other people's lives and careers. They caused their own downfall. They can't escape God's universal rule for everyone, "As a man sows; that will he also will reap." Every religion has some version of that law. It might take awhile, but it comes back around, how you treat people.*

It had been years she had anything to do with that case, so she spent two days in Judge Rosen's office reviewing the file to prepare for her deposition. They had a video tape recorder on her the entire time she reviewed the file.

"I don't know why I'm even reviewing this file; none of my stuff is in here." She said aloud, though no one answered her.

She started making a list of all of her notes that were missing. She had no idea what questions they would ask her in the deposition and she wanted to be as prepared as possible. Her handwritten notes, her interviews with the co-workers, so many things were gone. Several of the pictures from the homicide scene were gone from the file. There were no entries into her case notes from April 30th to May 12th. Twice she had entered those notes in this file, after they had disappeared the first time; then from the end of May to November, no entries from her investigation again. The file was thick; but it contained a lot of duplicated documents. There were over 20 PCR's in the file. There were notes from a Danny Marshall, that she didn't even remember being involved with the case. The two trips that she had taken to Ohio to interview her mother, the aunt in Georgia that she knew Godbold had visited, all of those interviews were missing from the file. It was like she had never touched the case. Her timeline wasn't even in there. She had created the timeline twice. Once when she started working the case and the other one after everything disappeared. The file had been compromised. *What a surprise….*

She took her oath, spent another two days of her life deposing with yet another pack of lawyers. She left Wayne County hoping she would never have to return, nor did she want to hear the names Kwame Kilpatrick or Tamara Greene again as long as she lived. The air just seemed fresher after the Wayne county line was in her rearview mirror.

Chapter 12.

Billy Jackson

Lieutenant Billy Jackson had worked for the Detroit Police Department since 1977. He was a seasoned officer by the time all the chaos started. He knew this was not going to end well long before he ended up getting demoted and working on patrol in squad 6. He was demoted the same day as Marian Stevenson.

It wasn't like he wanted to make everyone's life more difficult for the investigating officers by keeping the homicide file in his office. He was doing as he was commanded. He knew that all of this would come back to haunt them with the way that they were handling things.

The day the time bomb started ticking for this was the day Bowman met with the State Police about a possible connection between the cold-blooded murder of Tamara Greene on the streets of Detroit and some party supposedly hosted at the Manoogian mansion where a dancer got beat up by the mayor's wife.

He called Bowman into his office. "I need you to make three copies of the Tamara Greene homicide file. I also need copies of the report the Michigan State Police left including a list of any information they are asking for."

"Do you need them now?"

"Yes, I need them now. I have to take them to the Chiefs office for a meeting."

"Ok, I'm on it."

The copier was a piece of crap and kept miss-feeding the paper and breaking down, and the file was fairly thick, so it took a while to copy. Swartz called down multiple times asking what was taking so long, while Jackson helped Bowman with the copies; fixing the miss-feeds and trying to work with the faulty equipment.

He took the stack of papers and headed to the Chief's office. Bully-Cummings was quiet while Shwartz and Cueter asked him questions about what the Michigan State Police wanted and the questions that they had asked.

After he had answered all of their questions Schwartz looked at him and said, "Gather up all of the copies of the file. I want it kept in your office under lock and key. It is not to leave your office, do you understand? Under no circumstances is the file to leave your office."

He replied, "Absolutely. Yes, sir."

Then he gathered all of the copies of the file that he and Bowman had just made and took them back to his office and locked up for the day.

A few weeks later he was ordered take the case from Stevenson and give it to Godbold in cold case. Stevenson was having a hard time working on the case with the file in his office, but he knew she would be ticked when he told her it was being sent to cold case. She was still waiting for approval on her paperwork requesting to go to Alabama and interview Tamara's grandmother. From the weekly briefings they held, he knew she was still following leads.

He rang her extension and she answered immediately, "Stevenson here."

"Hi Marian, the Greene case has been moved to cold case."

Her voice was raised as she said, "What? You're kidding? I still have leads I'm working on."

"It's already been done. A cold case investigator will contact you if they have any questions about it."

Her tone was incredulous, "It isn't even two years old."

"Like I said, it's already done. You have other cases to work on, right?"

There was an awkward pause, "Yes, of course."

"Then you need to focus on those."

"Yes sir, is that all?"

That's all, have a good day."

"You too, sir."

He hung up the phone knowing that Godbold was going to have a fit when he learned that the file was to remain in his office under lock and key for at least thirty more days. What he didn't expect was for Godbold to have a fit when he was given the case.

Godbolds face got red when he informed him, "My nephew was screwing that bitch. I don't want this case."

"Well, it's yours. Take it up with cold case if you want it reassigned. You can reach Marian Stevenson at this number if you have any questions about where she was with it."

Godbold didn't look happy when he took Marian's card from his hand.

Jackson was getting ready to walk out of cold case, when he turned and said, "By the way, the file will be kept under lock and key in my office for at least thirty days. You can work on it over there. It is not to leave my office."

Godbold exploded, "You flipping have to be kidding me?!?"

"Watch your tone Godbold, here's my card, call me before you come over there so you can make sure I am in the office."

Godbolds lips were in a straight line and his face was fire-engine red, "Alright."

Over the next few weeks, Godbold had got into the habit of spending a few hours each day working in Jackson's office making notes about the case that would start his investigation. He still complained about the file being kept in his office, but Jackson ignored him. It wasn't his call. He was a man who followed orders. And Godbold didn't impress him all that much.

He was baby-sitting Godbold a few weeks later when he was told to transfer Bowman to the 6th precinct. He told Godbold he needed to leave his office for a few hours so he could conduct a meeting. Then he called Bowman into his office and offered him a seat. The chair he pointed to was stained and the plastic arms were cracked from years of use.

He knew that the only way to handle this was to be direct, "You're being transferred to the 6th precinct."

Bowman moved to the edge of his chair, "What are you talking about?"

"Effective immediately, you are being transferred."

Al Bowman looked confused; "Why are you sending me to precinct, I'm solving cases."

"You are also talking to the press and the state police. I am just doing what I was ordered to do. Al, you need to report to the 6th today."

"Today?"

"Just box up your stuff and head over there."

Bowman stood to his feet, "I think you're making a big mistake."

"I already told you Al, this wasn't my decision."

Bowman stood in the doorway, "Then there's nothing else to say."

"Shut the door on your way out."

Jackson stared at the closed door for a long time contemplating recent events. After 30 years as a cop, he had developed sharp instincts. His mind was like a calculator, it just kept adding everything up. The way Brown from Internal Affairs was fired for investigating the Executive Protection Unit, the interest from the brass in the murder investigation, the copies, the meetings, the "keep the file in your office under lock and key", the transfer of Bowman. He knew there was no way that it would not blow up in their faces someday. They were trying to cover up a steamy pile of dog shit in the middle of the living room floor with a paper towel.

His own demotion was a blessing when it came. It disassociated him from the events that were unfolding. He didn't want anything to do with it.

He knew that Marian Stevenson was getting ready to start interviewing the police officers that were present at the funeral just prior to the case being sent from homicide to cold case. The Reverend from the church deliberately brought the video to our office with a letter explaining why he thought it might be helpful to the case. Cops crawled all over the funeral. It wasn't like no one would notice them or recognize them. These people were not all that bright if they truly believed the tactics they were employing were a good idea or one that would work.

If they actually thought they could cover up the situation with intimidation and demotions of anyone who looked into it, they were idiots. Experience and instinct both set off the alarm bells in his head that screamed, *"Don't let them drag you into this. You are not going to jail for anybody."* The day he was demoted to the 6<sup>th</sup> precinct was indeed the best thing that could have happened. He was close to retiring and his pay grade was the same. When they sent him to the 6th, he didn't complain, he just went. On his time off, he scouted around until he found a fantastic place in Arizona to retire. After he secured the perfect home out west it would only be a matter of putting in time. His retirement day was circled with a red pen on every calendar he owned.

A few months prior to retiring he ran into Marian Stevenson while he was picking up a few things at Farmer Johns one Saturday morning. He saw her poking through a bin of avocados and noticed right away that she had lost some weight. She was thin before, but she was downright skinny now.

"Hey, Marian, fancy meeting you here."

She jumped, startled at his voice, "Hey Billy, how've you been?"

Smiling, he said, "Great, getting ready to retire and move to Arizona. How've you been doing?"

"Things have been better. I'm thinking about moving too."

She bit the ragged edge of her finger-nail. He looked at her hands, they were all nubs.

*Maybe she needs someone to talk to,* "I'd like to catch up if you have time. Want to go over to Starbucks and get some coffee?"

"That sounds good. I have to grab some spinach; then I can check out and meet you over there. Give me ten minutes."

He watched her push her cart to the refrigerated section of the store and pick up a bag of spinach before he turned and took his grapes and melons over to the check-out clerk. She was directly behind him, so he knew he wouldn't have to wait for her once he got to Starbucks. It wasn't like he had big plans for the day, but it was beautiful outside and he did want to get some yard work done that afternoon. It was supposed to rain Sunday.

He waited for her by the door and held it open as she walked in. Being a gentleman was second nature to him, he was taught to treat women with respect from the time he was a child. It was only at work that he adopted a military style; it was expected in that environment. Small gentlemanly actions could be easily misconstrued at work and viewed as unprofessional, especially with subordinates.

She ordered first and after he paid ten dollars for both of their coffees they found an empty café table by the window and sat down.

He looked at her with concern and asked her, "So what's been going on? Are you ok?"

"The last few years have been rough. Are you sure you want to hear it?"

The thought flashed through his mind, *she really does need to talk.* "That's why I'm here for coffee, Marian. I wanted to catch up, sometimes talking about things helps."

"When I got transferred over to the 9th, things started happening Billy, bad things. I'm working patrol in my own neighborhood and I've had four dispatch calls to my personal address with a complaint of an intruder that was armed and dangerous."

His eyebrows shot up, "Wow. Since you are sitting here talking to me, you obviously didn't respond."

"No, I didn't respond. It's worse than that, Billy. My house has been broken into three times, the first time my pistol was left laying in the middle of my bed. Someone keeps opening my front gate. I've been getting prank phone calls at 3 A.M. on and off for years now. I'm on anxiety medicine. It's made me a nervous wreck."

He reached across the table and took her small hand, "I can see why, I'm so sorry you have to go through this."

Big tears threatened to spill over her onto her cheeks. He knew that he was not looking at a weak woman.

She pulled her hand away from his grasp, and looked out of the window, "It's not your fault, Billy. I've never been one to run from anything, I grew up in this city. After twenty three years in my house and over twenty years on the police force, I'm considering leaving."

He looked at her kindly, "You know, Marian; you have nothing to be ashamed of. You did your time. You were a damn good investigator and had the highest conviction rate in homicide that I have ever seen."

She smiled at his kind words and replied, "You're right, we were a good team."

"We were a damn good team and don't you ever forget it. I know you believe in God, Marian and you need to remember something. There is a time and a season for everything that happens under heaven. Maybe it is just your time to move on."

She looked at him and smiled through her tears that had betrayed her by falling onto her cheeks, "Maybe you're right, maybe it is time to move on. I hear Arizona is nice."

"Arizona *is* nice. No grass to mow out there Marian, just an occasional cactus grows in the yard. I'm planning on putting in a stable and getting a few horses. Can you imagine me, a rancher?" He laughed and continued with a more serious tone, "The events of the last few years were not something that you could control. When you move, you can make a fresh start. Put all of this behind you and enjoy the rest of your life. You deserve that, Marian."

She knew he was right, but letting go was not an easy thing for her, "I love this city, Billy. I've spent my whole life here."

Then she smiled and told him, "You'll make an awesome rancher someday, I can totally see it."

He seemed to understand how she felt when he replied, "And you gave it your all. That's more than a most people in the department can say. If the stress is affecting your health, you need to do something about it."

She gave a half-laugh half-snort, "My doctor's been telling me the same thing for years."

He didn't seem surprised, "Maybe it's time you listened to him."

Nodding her head she said, "I agree; maybe even past time. It was good running into you today, Billy. The pep talk was timely and much needed."

He finished his fancy five dollar coffee in one gulp, "I enjoyed it too, Marian. I know you'll get things sorted out. You're a smart woman and you deserve the best. Better than what you got"

They stood at the same time and Marian gave him a timid hug. When she did he noticed again how thin she was, he felt her rib bones in his hands. She said, "I might not see you again before you leave to Arizona. Thanks for everything, Billy."

He held the door for her as she walked out, "Take care, Marian."

"You too, Billy. If I don't see you before you leave, have fun in Arizona." She replied, as she turned and headed toward her car.

After watching her get in and drive away, he made his way to his own car slowly thinking. *One thing about Stevenson, Bowman and I, after over 75 combined years as police officers, we can all hold our head high knowing that although we were demoted, we*

*left with our integrity. That counts for a lot in my book. Our*
*badges were untarnished.*

The next few months passed quickly for him. Packing for the movers and working out the details associated with retiring and moving kept him busy. He was retired and living in Arizona when he received a subpoena to depose in a lawsuit that claimed Detroit officials conspired to thwart the investigation into Tamara Greene's murder. He had known that this day would come.

To prepare for his deposition he reviewed the file. A lot of time had passed and he needed to refresh his memory with the details of the case to give a good deposition. He noticed several things that had been in the file when he was in possession of it were no longer there. His detective mind kicked in and he asked himself the following questions. Where did her funeral tape go? Where was Tamara's phone? Where did all the statements go that Stevenson took?

It was as if someone else had gone through the file and had done a separate investigation. Stevenson's time-line was missing. It was clear that a different person had done this time-line. The styles were not the same. There were a lot of duplicate papers and a lot of original investigation evidence, statements and interviews missing. The photos for the crime scene were photocopied and sparse. It didn't even resemble the file that he had turned over to cold-case before his demotion.

When reviewing the file past the date it had been turned over to the cold case division he noticed it odd that Godbold's entries were few and it looked like Tolbert had done all of the investigative work. *That isn't even right. Godbold and Lee worked on this case. If someone looked at this homicide file after it had gone to cold case, it would seem he did most of the footwork. They're still up to the same old tricks with this one. I'm ready to put this all behind me. I hope this is the last deposition they'll need from me.*

He hoped his deposition would help the case. *Tamara's family wants justice. That shouldn't be too much to ask. They deserve closure and even if they never find out who pulled the trigger, they are entitled to a proper investigation of her murder.*

*Where did the core values of truth and justice go? Or is this just how it is now?*

He left the deposition thinking how good it was to be retired. He thought about all the years he spent in Detroit and could draw no comparison with his life in Detroit and how much he loved living in Arizona. *I hope Marian found her happy place too. She deserves it. We all do.*

Chapter 13.

Odell Godbold

Retired Detroit Police Officer Odell Godbold was not thrilled

to be subpoenaed to be deposed regarding the Tamara Greene

murder investigation. He had been retired for five years now and

that case was the reason he left when he did. It was July 13, 2010

and it was a beautiful day. There were so many things he would

rather be doing than getting picked apart by lawyers all day long.

Yes, there was no doubt he would rather have been golfing. *Is*

*this case ever going to go away? I told them I didn't want the*

*damn case when they brought it to me. It wasn't even the fact that*

*my nephew was screwing her or that I had known the girl.*

*People talk, and people also had a history of getting demoted or*

*fired for touching the damn thing. My instincts were right. It*

*brought me nothing but problems from day one. I didn't need*

*that shit then and I don't need it now.*

With a long sigh he made the turn into the Bingham Farms

parking lot and prepared himself for another long day of

questions. He was ushered in to the well appointed office with high ceilings and a long polished conference table. The lawyers looked hungry, in their expensive black suits, as they readied for the deposition. They shuffled large stacks papers around in front of them with serious looks on their faces. It wasn't long before he was being sworn in to testify to the truth, the whole truth and nothing but the truth.

They took turns firing questions at him one after the other for hours:

Question: "Do you remember Tamara Greene's grandmother's name?"

He answered, "Christine White"

Question: "Did you or any of your investigators in cold case go down to Alabama and meet with Christine White?"

He reached for his coffee, "Yes, I think I went down – maybe August of '04. For maybe three days."

Question: "How many pages of notes did you take?"

"Five, six. I remember getting writing cramps."

Question: "Okay. What information useful to your investigation did you obtain on that first day?"

He rubbed his face with his hand and said, "Only that she had – the last time she had seen her was when she was en-route to Atlanta. She and another young lady stopped by and talked to her. Also that she had called her and had expressed some fears and she was fearful for her life, but she didn't go into details as to who that person or persons were that was invoking this fear in her, and a lot of other things that are here-say that I didn't put on paper."

Question: "Why didn't you put it on paper?"

His mind reacted to the question, *"This shit again?"* Then he answered, "At the time it had to do with the party and I didn't want to get into that. I was strictly focused on the homicide investigation."

Question: "When you say the party, what do you mean?"

He thought, *"Get off the damn party."* But his answer to their question was, "Well, she told me that Ms. Greene informed her that she had danced at the mansion and that there was a fight, things like that."

Question: "At the Manoogian mansion?"

"Yes."

Question: "Why weren't you interested at this time?"

"Because I didn't think that Ms. Greene was the target, I thought Eric Mitchell was the target, and I just wasn't concerned about whether she had danced or not."

Question: "You didn't feel that the Manoogian mansion party was relevant to Tamara Greene's death or her murder investigation?"

"That's Correct. It was not important to me, it was not my focus."

Question: "You Obtained information from Bryan Trumball as well concerning a dancer – I should say a police officer who's alleged to have been a dancer named Paytra Williams. Do you remember that?"

Sigh, "Yes."

Question: "Did you obtain that information from Trumball before or after you went to Alabama?"

"Before."

Question: "And the information you had been given was that Paytra Williams had danced and been injured at the mansion party. Correct?"

He takes another sip of coffee before he replies, "Yes."

Question: "And you actually interviewed Paytra Williams at some point, right?"

"Yes."

Question: "And she was scared when you spoke to her, correct?"

"Yes."

Question: Did you ever find out why she was scared?

*I didn't care why she was scared.* "No, I told her. I don't want to hear this. Okay. Just keep your mouth shut, and that was the gist of the conversation."

Question: "And the "this" you are referring to was her dancing at the Manoogian mansion party correct?"

"Yes. As I reflect back, I believe that Donald Hughes was a mole. He was aware of the fact that I interviewed Officer Williams and he was aware of the fact that we discussed things, and I believe Donald conveyed that information to Tolbert."

Question: "What do you mean a 'mole'?"

*What the hell do they think a mole is?* He answered, "Placed there to monitor our activities on Ms. Greene case. No one could touch Don and that was the talk of the homicide section. I knew he was carrying information to Tolbert, and to Tolbert's bosses Assistant Chief Walt Martin and Deputy Chief Saunders."

Question: "Who reported directly to Chief of Police Ella Bully-Cummings?"

"Correct."

Question: "Were you aware there was a video in the homicide file of the funeral?"

"Yes."

Question: "Did you see anyone you recognized in that videotape?"

"I believe there were a couple of police officers that I recognized."

Question: "As you sit here today do you know who those individuals are?"

*Why do I have to be dragged into this?* He answered, "I know who they are now, but couldn't tell you if I ran into them. I don't know what they look like. I just know they were part of the Mayors extra protection."

Question: "The Executive Protection Unit, right?"

"Yes."

Question: "And they were a part of that protection unit back in 2003 at the time Tamara Greene was killed, right?"

"Yes."

Question: "Did Sergeant Stevenson ever tell you they were on the videotape?"

"I don't recall her telling me that, no."

Question: "Was the video in the file of Judge Rosen's office when you reviewed the file?"

"I didn't see it, no."

Question: "In your two discussions with Sergeant Marian Stevenson, did she ever relate to you that she was getting ready to turn her focus toward people on the mayoral staff?"

*That's why I ended up with the case,* "She did tell me that, yes."

Question: "And what was your response to her?"

Another sip of the coffee, great, it had gone cold. "I didn't have any.....I had no response to her."

Question: "Did you make notes of this that you put in the file?"

"No."

Question: "Do you believe Lieutenant Tolbert was trying to impede your investigation of Tamara Greene's murder?"

"Yes. The fact that they did not allow cold case ample time to investigate Ms. Greene's case – under the pretense of reassigning me to a new unit. To investigate some people squad six was already investigating. So, I knew then they were throwing up roadblocks, if you will, to stop this investigation. That was my feeling. I went over to the Federal- Fisher building around

November of '04 and that there was no need for me to come to headquarters. I was at headquarters on one occasion and Deputy Chief Saunders approached me and said, "What are you doing here?" I said, "I came to talk to cold case, you know." He told me, "No, I don't want you coming over here. Get back to the Fisher Building."

Question: "So effectively they shut down the cold case investigation of Tamara Greene in November of 2004, haven't they?"

"Yes. I was still the officer in charge of the case and I had no access to the physical file, it was at headquarters and I was told not to go there. They had me in the basement of the Fisher building without even a computer down there to use."

Question: "You describe unexplained hostility from your superiors; can you explain in as much detail as possible what kinds of hostility you were experiencing at the time?"

The thought flashed through his mind, *Would you like that in book format?* But he answered honestly, "Well, I would meet with Assistant Chief Martin and it was always profanity filled, hostile tone. I just couldn't understand it, especially in a professional environment. For instance, he wanted me to – he said I was a piss-poor supervisor because I couldn't get my officers to pay for out of town travel out of their own pockets. I mean, that's ludicrous."

Question: "That is not department policy, is it?"

"Absolutely not."

Question: "And then you indicate that cold case was shut down, what do you mean?"

"I came to work one morning and the whole office was empty. Desks removed, computers removed, cabinets removed, completely bare. I approached Tolbert and he told me cold case was being shut down indefinitely. I asked, "Can you give me a reason why?" I couldn't understand that because we were successful at what we were doing. Cold case helped their statistics, yea- end statistics with the case we were closing. But he couldn't give me an answer, he just said, you are going to be reassigned to squad 6."

Question: "Do you have any idea why it was shut down?"

"I believe it was to protect officer Williams and others."

Question: "And who do you believe was trying to protect officer Williams?"

"Assistant Chief Walt Martin. He came from internal affairs and it's only speculation and may be classified as heresy, but belief in the department was that (then) inspector Martin initiated the sequence of events that led to the Gary Brown incident. When Brown was demoted and fired by Mayor Kilpatrick for his investigation of the overtime abuse and allegations of assault being committed at the mansion. It's only what you hear. And so I believe he is- he was- the key reason..Well, Tolbert couldn't shut down cold case that had to come from higher up. It had to come from the assistant Chief or the chief, and I think Assistant Chief Martin shut down cold case in order to protect Officer Williams and/or others. It opened back up in 2006 after my retirement."

Question: "And was the shutting down of cold case part of the reason you ultimately decided to retire from the Detroit Police Department?"

"I felt that – and it's only based on my experience as an investigator that there was a conspiracy to undermine the integrity of the – of Ms. Greene's investigation. I wanted no part of it, and if you wear that badge, you wear it with integrity and I wasn't going to tarnish my badge, no."

Question: "And because of that you retired?"

"Yes."

Question: "And the individuals you believe were behind that conspiracy to impede the investigation were Tony Saunders, Walt Martin and James Tolbert?"

"Yes."

Question: "Can you list some of the items you noticed may have been missing from the Tamara Greene homicide file when you reviewed it in Judge Rosen's office?"

His stomach growled and he wondered; *when are these people going to take a lunch break? A lot of items were missing from the file.* As hungry as he was, he tried to concentrate.

He answered them as thoroughly as he could, "Handwritten progress notes from me and Erika Lee, Tamara's phone, the funeral video, interviews that were there from our trip to Ohio to interview her family, notes from our trip to Alabama to interview her grandmother, any reference to any police officer being at her funeral. Written statements from the bartender where Ms. Greene worked. Some items that were on the evidence list were not in the file. It had been compromised. "

Question: How crucial a piece of evidence in the investigation of Tamara Greene's death was this cell phone?

"Extremely crucial... yes. It would give us a record of calls received, calls going out, whom she called prior to the tragedy, address list, contacts, yes, it was crucial. The phone was on the evidence list, but it never came with the file to cold case, so that had been missing prior to the case coming to me. Stevenson, she had claimed to me that she had a lot of things come up missing while she was working the case, and her computers had been messed with, case notes erased. We did a lot of duplicate work on the case, and upon the inspection of the file prior to this deposition, my case notes are also missing."

It went on and on. It was an excruciatingly long day of questioning. Odell Godbold was hungry and tired when the deposition was over and he could finally get out of there. He never wanted anything to do with that case from the day they pushed it on him. He didn't owe anyone anything. There was no reason, at his age, to have to put up with what he put up with. Especially at that point in his career, he had been close to retiring. That stint they made him pull in the basement without a computer was humiliating.

Glad to be retired, he drove home and fixed himself a drink with shaky hands. *They can all get in a conga line and kiss my ass.* He sat down in his recliner, kicked it back to the lounge position and said to the empty room, "As far as I am concerned, this is over.

**A final word from the author:**

Yes, it makes a good story, this urban legend. It has every ingredient necessary. If someone removed 250 pieces of a 1000 piece puzzle, a person with tenacity and dedication could still put enough of it together to get the picture.

The delay, obfuscation, malfeasance and criminal acts that occurred among high ranking officials in the investigations regarding Tamara's murder, was nothing short of staggering. People who deem themselves above the law, do not want her murderer found. It would be difficult to come to a different conclusion with the volume of testimony, affidavits, text messages, and missing evidence. Combined with the wrongful demotion/termination of detectives all taken into account, it creates a horrific picture of corruption.

Those familiar with the Tamara Greene case will recognize that (one) part of this story was purely fiction, please allow me to clarify:

- She had three children, not one, as depicted in the story. Two of her children are still minors.

The Michigan State Police and Michigan Attorney General investigation was not included in this book for the following reasons:

- They were investigating the party only, not the murder of Tamara Greene

- Mike Cox refused to document or to record the interview when he questioned Kwame Kilpatrick about the party.

- Mike Cox did not allow Michigan State Police Officers to attend that meeting, under protest of the investigating officers, which circumvented protocols.

- Ruth Carter, Detroit Judge, asked the mayor through a series of text messages if he would prefer to be cleared by Mike Cox or Dugan from the Michigan State Police, prior to the questioning happening.

If the Detroit Police Department is finished playing musical chairs; and wants to solve the murder of Tamara Greene, please feel free to start with the questions that I have:

- Who were the police officers in attendance at the funeral and how did they know Tamara Greene?

- Were any of the officers that were at the scene of her murder in attendance of her funeral?

- Can Nextel or Sprint be subpoenaed for the final phone bill of Tamara Greene?

- Why would someone move an officer out of homicide who solved ninety seven percent of her cases, and who made that decision?

- Why wasn't due process followed in the transfers and demotions of the detectives that worked on this case?

- Why was a murder case moved to cold case that still had active leads that were being investigated?

- Why were protocols circumvented as it related to the handling of physical evidence in a murder investigation?

- Who obstructed this murder investigation by removing items from the file?

- How did Christine Beatty receive a copy of the first memo regarding the investigation of the party and improprieties of the Executive Protection Unit prior to the Police Chief?

- Who do the security cameras on the floor by her office show as delivering the document under her door?
- Can an IT expert retrieve case notes from the DPD server and reconstruct a particular day?

***

My personal insurance policy is the fact that if I, or any member of my family, suffer any harm or perceived harm from writing this book, there will be consequences:

- Ten copies of a document containing my personal conclusions about this case are securely maintained in diverse locations and will be distributed to the media and the internet both simultaneously and immediately.
- Names of people that may be involved with this case that aren't included in this book are included in those documents. Including enough evidence to support an investigative inquiry of my claims.

**Corruption exists because it is tolerated.**

***

Ten percent of the proceeds of this book will be put into an account for the children of Tamara Greene.

***

References.

1. Tamara Greene feared for her life, reverend says in affidavit, Detroit Free Press, 3/19/2008
2. Former police clerk says she saw stripper's police report of Manoogian assault, Grand Rapids Press, 3/11/2008
3. Douglas Bayer, EMT, whistleblower lawsuit
4. Lt. Walter Godzwon, EMS Supervisor, affidavit
5. Cenobio Chapa, EMS paramedic, affidavit
6. Sandy Cardenas: Retired Police Dispatched, affidavit states she sent several police cars to a disturbance at the Manoogian mansion in the fall of 2002. She also stated that internal affairs officers showed up and confiscated the tapes.
7. Marian Stevenson, deposition, 6/18/2010
8. Odell Godbold, deposition, 4/26/2010
9. Billy Jackson, deposition
10. Alvin Bowman, deposition, 8/5/2010
11. Gary Brown, deposition, 7/22/2010
12. Jerry Oliver, deposition, 8/11/2010
13. Harold Nelthrope, deposition, 8/2/2010
14. Norman Yatooma: Detroit city attorney said I could, 'end up with a knife in my back' for deposing Bernard Kilpatrick in stripper lawsuit, Detroit News, 3/24/2010
15. Firing of Gary Brown had set off alarms, Beatty ordered secret seizure of files, cops recall, AP, 3/27/2008

16. Gary Brown on Tamara Greene investigation: Basic Investigative techniques not followed, MLive, 10/6/2009

17. Urban Legend or is it more? City workers claim they were punished for investigating Manoogian mansion party, Click on Detroit, 11/17/2011

18. Texts cast light on Manoogian probe, City's top lawyer talked to AG Cox, 3/10/2009

19. Cox denies attending stripper party with Kwame Kilpatrick, AP, 7/27/2010

20. Stripper says she danced at Manoogian Mansion, saw Carlita Kilpatrick assault Tamara Greene, AP, 11/22/2010

21. Cop who investigated Tamara Greene death will take bosses to court, Detroit News, 1/16/2013

22. Who Killed Tamara Greene?, Detroit News, 3/14/2008

23. Detroit Cops win $6.5M Suit Against Mayor, CBS/AP, 6/3/2010

24. Detroit pair get $6.5M in whistleblower case, Ex-officers' suit alleged misdeeds by mayor, staff, AP, 9/12/2007

25. The Chain of Events, Detroit Free Press, 1/24/2008

26. Racy texts contradict testimony from Detroit mayor, aide, CNN Politics.com, 1/24/2008

27. Brown vs. Mayor of Detroit, Docket Nos. 259911,259923 – 7/27/2006

28. Lover of former Detroit Mayor admits guilt, Christine Beatty admits to obstruction of justice, AP, 12/2/2008

29. Read newly unsealed testimony in Tamara Greene lawsuit (foul language), Detroit Free Press, 1/10/2012

30. Internal Affairs? One time cops allege they were ousted and harassed because they knew of Mayor Kilpatrick's "Philandering", Metro Times, 5/26/2004

31. Christine Beatty testifies by teleconference in Tamara Greene lawsuit, ABC action news, 3/23/2011

32. Read Kilpatrick's and Beatty's text messages, Judge orders release of key documents in whistle-blower case, Detroit Free Press, 4/29/2008

33. Ex-Detroit cop in probe of strippers death can sue bosses, AP, 1/16/2013
34. Lawyer: Calls from city-issued cell phones on slain stripper's phone?, ABC, 8/22/2010

Made in the USA
Columbia, SC
22 December 2023

29349227R00133